First published in 2018

DARK CASTLE
PRESS

CONTENTS

VIKING

WOLF

EMMANUELLE
DE MAUPASSANT

NOTES FROM THE AUTHOR

Welcome to my 'Viking Warriors' steamy romance series.

I hope you enjoy 'Viking Wolf', and its prequel 'Viking Thunder'.

The story concludes with 'Viking Beast'.

Svolvaen and Skálavík are fictitious, as are my characters. While the superstitions and rituals related in this series are based on true Norse beliefs, I've taken liberties in shaping them. The *draug* (a restless spirit which reanimates its human form), I've adapted to suit the needs of my tale. You'll recognize the Norse myths, though with many omissions and told with my own emphasis.

Daily life and habits in Svolvaen are based on my research, some of which is drawn from the 'Hurstwic' online site. I've described the longhouse much as we believe it would have appeared, with deep benches along each interior wall (used for sitting and sleeping). Central firepits provided warmth and a means of cooking, with smoke drawn through a hole in the roof. While it's commonly believed that most longhouses were 'windowless', the sagas of *Brennu-Njáls* and *Grettis* both mention openings akin to windows (without glass but using skins which could be drawn back). I've used this device, as it serves my plot.

For the purpose of this story, Eirik and Gunnolf's beds are situated at either end of the longhouse, being 'boxed' in wood, to offer more privacy.

CAST

Brought from Northumbria, by Eirik
Elswyth – newly widowed, former wife of Holtholm's chieftain, now Eirik's lover
Faline – Elswyth's stepdaughter

Svolvaen residents
Gunnolf ('fighting wolf') – chief of Svolvaen and Eirik's older brother
Eirik ('eternal ruler') – brother to Gunnolf
Asta - Gunnolf's wife
Helka – sister to Eirik and Gunnolf
Guðrún and Sylvi – Gunnolf's thralls (slaves who undertake household duties)
Astrid – a village woman who befriends Elswyth
Ylva - Astrid's daughter
Torhilde – Astrid's neighbour
Bodil – a former lover of Eirik
Anders – the blacksmith
Halbert – the blacksmith's son

Olaf – friend to Eirik

<u>Deceased</u>
Wyborn ('war bear') - father to Eirik, Helka and Gunnolf
Wybornsson
Hallgerd – the previous jarl (uncle to Eirik, Helka and Gunnolf)
Vigrid – Helka's first husband

<u>Bjorgyn residents</u>
Jarl Ósvífur
Leif Ósvífursson – oldest son of Jarl Ósvífur
Freydís Ósvífursdóttir – sister to Leif

<u>Skálavík residents</u>
Jarl Eldberg (the Beast)

1

---

959 AD

With the midsummer sun dipping to the last portion of the sky, twenty men pulled the oars.

We were three days on the open sea, travelling to Svolvaen. As the boat battled the wind, my stomach heaved with the churning of the waves. My thoughts turned repeatedly to my grandmother, lying weak in her bed, left in the care of the other women of our village. My decision had been selfish. I yearned for adventure and the chance to start anew but, most of all, I was governed by my desire for Eirik—the leader of these Northmen who'd been cast onto our rocky coastline.

How scared I was, sick with fear and the motion of the vessel. Eirik pulled me to him, murmuring comforts. I was grateful for his strength, as I struggled with my own weakness.

At last, we sighted the mountains of the north. Reaching the calmer waters of their coast, sailing between scattered islands, the men's gaze raked the maze of inlets, looking for their own. Gulls and gannets whirled above as we followed a narrow channel, past cliffs on either side, pocketed with caves.

Horns blew through the still dusk of the evening as we approached the landing piers, where other ships were tethered. I shared in the crew's elation, for I was now part of this world, although all in it would be new to me.

There was a press of bodies: comradery between men, kisses from wives, embraces from mothers, daughters and sisters. In those women's faces, I recognized myself for, like them, I was tall and golden-haired, sharing their Norse blood.

Amidst the jumble of voices and the scramble of the crowd, Faline and I received little regard. We were no more than possessions, of Eirik's concern alone. Whatever welcome I'd hoped for in my heart, whatever foolishness, I pressed it down and bit my tongue against disappointment. To earn my place would take time.

Eirik's sister, Helka, guided us away and we climbed the slope rising from the small harbour. The modest dwellings we passed appeared little different from those of my own village, comprising low walls of stone, their roofs turfed. The light had almost gone as we approached the summit of the hill, where stood a longhouse of great size. A sentry guarded either side of its door, whom Eirik greeted with clasped hands.

The vaulted ceiling rose higher than that of the home I'd not long ago shared with my husband. The ribs reached up into the darkness, above a central fire pit. The flames leapt, smoke curling upwards, to an open hole in the roof. The air was thick with the smell of stew, for a great cauldron hung over the heat of the pit. Along the length of the hall were deep benches with sheepskins upon them, providing room enough to sleep the household and many more.

Upon a raised dais sat a man and woman richly dressed, who I took to be the chieftain of their village, or *jarl* in their own tongue, and his fair wife. The pale beauty had an air of delicate refinement, her fine hair hanging to her waist. She wore a silvered cloak complimenting her dress of light-blue. Her husband's garb was raven-black, and he sported a beard and mane just as dark. In the half-light, the shadows played over his face.

Faline and I stood behind Helka, who whispered a little of what was said, translating enough for us to understand. I was glad, too, that during our sea voyage, Eirik had begun to teach me some of his words.

"Jarl Gunnolf, and my Lady Asta." Eirik bowed.

"You're returned then, brother." Gunnolf shared Eirik's full lips and strong jaw, and he bore a livid scar through one eyebrow, deeper than that crossing Eirik's cheek. Despite the white creeping at his temples, he appeared in his prime, and there was a concentrated intensity to him.

I made myself lower my eyes.

"Helka, dear sister." Gunnolf rose from his seat, approaching us. "You've brought prizes, I see."

Grasping above my elbow, he looked at me directly. His eyes were the same icy blue as Eirik's, and my own. His scrutiny was piercing, as if penetrating to my naked skin.

Abruptly, he unhooked my cloak, letting it fall, so that I stood in my worsted dress. His eyes took in the shape of me and lingered in careful appraisal.

With a shake of her dark hair, Faline jostled forward, pushing back her cloak to reveal the curves of her young body, wishing to capture the jarl's attention for herself.

He regarded her with some amusement before resuming his examination of me.

Eirik moved closer to my side, placing his hand firmly upon my shoulder. "Elswyth is a woman of former standing, and with some proficiency in healing." His voice, though level, was firm. "She is mine."

Gunnolf's eyes narrowed, and I saw him set his jaw as he

squared his shoulders to Eirik. His fist clenched and I feared he'd reach for the dagger at his belt. The vein at Eirik's temple stood visible as he returned his brother's glare.

The two stood silent for some moments, before the tension broke, and Gunnolf's mouth twitched in a half-smile. His gaze returned to Faline. "And this one?"

Eirik answered with all courtesy. "Elswyth's cousin. Both I offer for Asta's service, if our Lady wishes it. They come as free women but are willing to serve."

It was as we had agreed. I would need some occupation besides the tumbling companion of mighty Eirik, and my duties would be light, he assured me.

"For that, my Lady thanks you," said Gunnolf, replying for his wife. "No doubt, they will bend to the command of their betters, for all that you call them 'free.'"

Gunnolf then pulled Eirik close and whispered in his ear. They laughed, clasping each other about the back. However, as Gunnolf pressed his cheek to his brother's shoulder, his expression was without mirth. If it was joy he felt at Eirik's return, it was soberly tempered.

As Eirik led me away, I felt the jarl's inscrutable gaze upon us.

2

Eirik carried me to his bed, which would now be mine, in the service of our mutual pleasure. He cared not for the others, who would surely hear us beyond the meagre curtain of our boxed chamber, and nor did I. He lay me back, freeing his erection from the rough wool of his trousers.

The hard-muscled ridges of his abdomen led to the thatch of his groin, and the thick root of his manhood. His size was enough to awe any woman, but I was eager. My cream trickled wet, in anticipation of receiving him. I wanted to feel the insistence of his hands and his mouth, and to be coated with the sweat of his body.

"Warm and tight, my Elswyth." Eirik drew up my legs and breached me. "And so very ready. What have you been thinking of all this time? How you would take my cock into you, and milk me of my seed? How you would spread your legs wide, and beg me to fuck harder?

I caught my breath as he gave me his full length, filling my sheath beyond what I had ever thought possible. Eyes bright with desire, he began his steady rhythm.

I could not contain my moans as his thrusts grew harder. He

pulled me upwards to meet those fierce lunges. With the force of his fucking, my voice rose. I'd known his need would be violent, and I welcomed it. At last, his voice broke in a Viking oath, and he shuddered. His final plunge brought a pulsing flood. I gave my own cry—part pain and joy.

From the body of the main hall, beyond our chamber, came sounds of laughter and lewd comment. I was shamed, in part, by this lack of privacy, yet also pleased—for there would be no doubt in others' minds that I pleased Eirik.

With a low chuckle, Eirik lowered his mouth to mine, kissing me softly.

"A good beginning, my Elswyth." His hands moved upwards, first to squeeze my waist, then to push down the fabric covering my breasts. He took each in his mouth, humming low, rubbing his beard where it would most antagonize me.

I wriggled, and clenched around his engorgement, knowing that it wouldn't be long before he was again ready.

Hurriedly, he pulled off my gown and the shift beneath, so that I lay naked. Stretched back on the bed, I opened my legs to him, awakened to desire and the certainty of fulfilment.

When his own clothing was removed, he knelt low above me, and I quivered at the sight of him. I knew all the scars of his body, and its cloak of ink. There were the intricate patterns upon his arms, dark green and blue, forming the branches of knotted trees. A snake curved down his spine, whose scales rippled as he moved. Its twisted head, placed over Eirik's shoulder, seemed to watch me. I pressed my palm to the circle of arrows on his chest.

His erection was already rising.

He circled my nipple lightly, then trailed downward, over the curve of my belly. He stroked through my soft fur, dipping the tip of one finger to my parted slit. With tortuous gentleness, he teased there, pressing and retreating, and my wetness grew.

I writhed, lifting my hips to meet his caress, and all the while he looked into my eyes. I held his gaze, wanting this connection between us—for him to see me.

"With just my finger, little bird, I can trap you and keep you, or make you fly." His voice growled low, speaking in my own language, his vowels drawn out as he formed the words. 'With my tongue, I can take you to the doors of Valhalla."

Raising my hips again, he lowered his face, brushing my delicate skin with the bristles of his beard. He drew the flat of his tongue through my slit, before flicking against the sensitive point.

It was as I desired, his tongue working to bring me to another peak. He took the swollen flesh hard into his mouth, suckling there as if the nub were another nipple, and he a babe seeking nourishment. My cream flowed for him, and he drank it eagerly.

Yet, all the while, he kept me upon the edge.

"Please," I begged, "Eirik…"

"More?" His breath was hot against my thigh.

I bit my lip as he penetrated more deeply with his tongue, stroking upwards upon each retreat.

He lifted his head and grinned, emerging from my slipperiness.

When he sat back on his heels, I reached for him, eager to pull him down and into me. However, he took both my hands and moved them to the base of his meat.

"Feel me," he said. "Take it. Taste it."

Gripping the shaft, I rolled the skin back and forth, before guiding him to my lips. Being careful with my teeth, I moved over his smoothness, beyond the furrow and some way down his column. I sucked upon his length, enclosing him tightly. I loved the solidity of him in my mouth.

He shifted and groaned, pushing one of my hands lower to cover his sac. He closed his fingers over mine, rubbing himself through my grasp, kneading at his own heaviness. At last, I extended my fingers to caress the skin between his balls and his anus.

"Völva!" he groaned, calling me an enchantress, twisting under the pleasure I gave him.

I smiled as I took him from my mouth, for I fully intended to bewitch him. Shifting quickly, I moved to sit astride his lap. I was ready to lose myself in the heat of his body, but the devil in me wished him to wait, as I had waited.

I was open, slick with his semen and my own desire, but I held back, rubbing only the tip of him to my ache.

"Now!" He growled, pulling me down so that he slid inside in one deep stroke.

Burying his face in my breasts, he pulled a nipple into his mouth, tugging hungrily, grazing me with his teeth.

"Faster!" Eirik's hands were firm on my waist. Impatiently, he took control, lifting me bodily up and down upon his shaft.

As my tumult crashed upon me, Eirik pressed his fingers between my cheeks, pushing me to take him deeper. Three more strokes and his head fell back. His eyes were wide and glassy, his mouth open in breathlessness. His cock leapt inside me and my own terrible delight swept me into the dark chasm.

I lay in the curve of Eirik's back, listening to the wind rise. I'd once told Helka that I was filled with longing for something I couldn't name; that I felt I'd die for want of it. Had I found what I was looking for, or had my search only just begun?

3

The barley ripened in the heat, dipping in the lazy winds of late summer.

Eirik was a warrior leader of his Viking raiders, but a farmer too, toiling alongside his men to harvest the crop. With their muscle-corded arms and broad shoulders, they were built like oxen: necks thick, and bodies used to labor.

As the afternoon sun retreated, I would walk out to find Eirik in the fields. Among the scent of hay, freshly bundled, stacked beneath a blue sky, I would taste his sweat and the brine of his cock. I gave myself, in whichever way pleased him.

His men grew accustomed to our habit, slapping him upon the back at my approach, sharing bawdy comments. They nodded to me, in friendly fashion, for I made Eirik happy, and he was well-loved among his men.

Svolvaen was a fertile place, rich in apple orchards, pears and cherries. Vegetables grew in abundance. There was good pasture for livestock. Its people seemed to work for the good of all, without the jealousies and disagreements of my former home.

Gunnolf's methods of keeping law were both strict and fair. A man caught stealing pork from the smokehouse was bidden to eat only from the trough for a week and to sleep with the pigs. It caused much merriment among the men, as well as having the desired effect upon the miscreant. He was duly humiliated: a punishment worse than any whiplashing.

The jarl had a quick tongue and a temper to match, which he made no effort to curb. Those who showed their fear received his scorn. Where our paths crossed, I held my head high, refusing to give him the satisfaction of dominating me. Whatever attraction I felt, I pushed it to one side, for I had no wish to tread where my feet should not step.

My nature did not bend easily to service, despite the submission I'd endured while wed to Faline's father. However, I found it no trial to wait upon Lady Asta, who was all gentleness.

She was carrying a child but, with many months ahead, she was able to attend herself in most matters. We did little more than heat the water for her bath and care for her wardrobe. Faline bristled under her diminished status, having been raised with servants of her own. Not being born to luxuries, I was more easily content, though my position had changed greatly since I'd sat at the left hand of my chieftain, with others to wait upon me.

Asta enjoyed our lively companionship, and we passed many hours in braiding her hair. Sitting under the sun's warmth, the jarl's wife patiently taught us more of her language and customs.

There was no need for me to dirty my hem in the pigsty, nor to labor in the skinning of game for our stew. I knew how to tend livestock, and to cook, but these were Guðrún and Sylvi's duties. Nonetheless, I helped in small ways, for it seemed wrong to set myself above them.

With Asta's permission, I sometimes milked the goats and cows, or churned the butter. Eirik said the cheeses I made were the best he'd tasted. With Sylvi, I went down to the shore to harvest dulse; the seaweed brought a briny tang to the fish stew she was adept at making. I learnt to preserve meat in vats of sour whey to prevent it from spoiling. I hung herring in the smokehouse, or outdoors, to dry in the brisk, northern wind. I refilled the lamps each morning with fish oil, adding cottongrass long enough for the wick.

I took on the language of my new home, word by word. Soon, I was reading my neighbours not only by their expressions–which were mostly of curiosity, though sometimes of pity or scorn–but by the phrases I began to unravel.

I wondered how many years it would take for them to accept me, to look into my eyes and not see a stranger. I had Viking blood, violently conceived during a raid by Northmen more than twenty years ago, but I hadn't been raised as one of them. Their rituals and habits were not yet mine, but I wished to learn. For too long, I'd fought with the knowledge of not belonging.

The women of Svolvaen regarded Faline and I with envy, I could tell, for we enjoyed comparative leisure. They treated us with a certain reverence, too, for Lady Asta was respected and loved, and she desired that others make us welcome.

"Her father was a jarl," Helka told me, "And his before. The marriage brought alliance with a settlement further north. She came with a rich dowry, of golden-threaded gowns, and cuffs and rings set with gemstones traded from the East."

Even without her jewels and fine costume, she was a woman above all others: regal, self-possessed, and beautiful. It was my pleasure to serve her and my fortune for, day by day, I came to love her.

Despite his wife's condition, or perhaps because of it, Gunnolf left Asta alone much of the day. When he did visit, he was attentive, asking after her comfort and placing his palm upon her belly. There was no doubt that he desired the son he believed was to be born. He laughed in her company, as her sweet voice related some household tale, or sang gently. He was wont to lay his head upon her lap, his eyes closed as she stroked his hair. With her, he sought to be cherished, rather than feared.

However, he was like other men, with an eye that too often roamed to young women of good flesh and reasonable looks. He seemed well able to separate love from desire. Perhaps, it had always been that way, and Asta was able to accept his nature, without thinking any less of Gunnolf or of herself. She never spoke a word against him.

He made little effort to conceal his gaze, oft watching as I carried out my modest duties. I'd no wish to fall prey to his lasciviousness. He reminded me of a lone wolf I'd encountered as a child. I'd swiftly climbed a tree and it had appraised me from below, as if deciding whether I was worth the trouble of acquiring.

I found the jarl regularly with Guðrún or Sylvi, taking one or the other—up against the wall, or outside, barely concealed—while his wife was elsewhere, growing his child in her belly.

I felt sure that Faline was playing a game with the master of the house, allowing herself to be taken, but upon her own terms. As she served his mead and meat, Faline brushed her breast against his arm and nudged him with her hip. She would dart away, to watch him coolly, from Asta's side, wetting her lips as he surveyed her, twitching with suppressed desire.

If Asta knew, she did not betray it. Rather, she readily came to Faline's defense. "Don't be angry with her. Some things are best let go, lest our bitterness eat us from within," Asta said, on hearing me rail against Faline's laziness.

Of my worse suspicions, I said nothing.

I had not her generosity of spirit, though I admired it. In the days that were to come, I thought often of Asta's serenity, and tried to emulate it, in the face of what I was unable to change. I coveted the respect given to her, and yearned for the dignity it would accord me to be Eirik's wife. I wished for all to know that he valued me above any other woman. There had been many, of that I had no doubt.

Though I spoke nothing of these quiet resentments, I couldn't resist asking Asta of the ceremonies that accompanied a man's joining to a woman in marriage. She knew, I supposed, that I alluded to my own hopes. She lowered her eyes and gave only the briefest of descriptions, seeming reluctant to dwell on the details I craved.

Perhaps she sensed, even then, that my wish to wed Eirik would bring me pain.

I was walking through the village one afternoon, when I came upon the younger children in their play. Some were afraid of me; others laughed to hear me speak. I wondered when I might have my own child—for Eirik to carry upon his shoulders, and who would grow up to belong.

So far, my bleeding came as it always did, and my belly remained flat.

A boy of no more than two toppled and scraped his knee. With a howl, he ran to his mother, seated nearby, and buried his face in her skirts. He stretched to request the comfort of her lap, but she held a baby. There was no room for both.

I stepped forward, offering my own arms, for the baby had finished its feed. However, she chivvied her son to run along. Perhaps, it was his renewed wail that made her reconsider, or she saw the shadow of hurt cross my face.

Relenting, she beckoned me to sit beside her, and passed the dozing babe into the crook of my elbow. She then lifted the boy to her lap.

How beautiful the baby was, pale lashes resting upon rounded cheeks. I wondered how it would feel for those lips, pursed in sleep, to suckle at my own breast. My heart ached with the need to hold my own child.

"I'm Astrid." The woman shifted the weight of the boy, who'd ceased his weeping and was now peering at me.

I smiled in return and gave my name. I praised the health of her baby and her little boy, and we fell into halting conversation. She was more than ten years older than I, and her aspect was weary, but she remained an attractive woman. She had, but recently, become a widow, for her husband had been among those of Eirik's raiding party who had not returned.

The news pained me, for I remembered the day on which I'd tended the wounds of those men and had seen Eirik's grief for his comrades lost. There were women of my former home, too, who'd lost their husbands—at the hands of Eirik's fearsome band. How fruitless such violence was.

"Eirik has been good to us, giving us some of his own livestock." Astrid sighed. "I would remarry, but there are few men for the women here." She regarded me silently for a while before closing her eyes, rocking the toddler against her shoulder.

The baby had just begun to stir when a young woman appeared behind Astrid, letting her mother know that she'd go to the lower meadow to bring back their goats from grazing.

"You're a good girl, Ylva." Astrid stroked her daughter's arm. "Keep on your shawl, remember, and hurry back."

I couldn't help but wonder at the linens Ylva had wrapped closely around her neck, for it was a fine day, and warm.

Astrid looked at me once more, and the infant I held—now balling its fists to its eyes and stretching in wakefulness. She slipped her boy to the ground, sending him to play, and reached to take the baby from me.

Her face was pale as she spoke. She was uneasy, but I sensed her desire to unburden herself, and speaking such things is sometimes easier with a stranger. There was no one near but she lowered her voice, nonetheless.

"My daughter woke with a sore upon her shoulder several days ago. Now, there are two more, about her throat."

I listened with concern. I'd seen my grandmother treat various skin ailments. I leaned forward, telling Astrid of my skill, and that I might be able to help. She appeared disbelieving though, doubtless, she would wish my claim to be true.

"I've given offerings to Eir, washed the pus with mead, and applied honey. It seems only to have grown worse."

I commended her on her actions, but I was anxious, for I feared that the sore would spread its poison through her daughter's body. Moreover, contact might spread the affliction to others in the family.

"Will Ylva let me see, tomorrow, if I return?" I had already begun to think of remedies I might try, and which combinations of plants would be most effective. "I'll bring a salve, and we must hope for a cure. I'll do all I can."

Astrid smiled uncertainly. "She'll do as I bid her."

I rose to take my leave but had one more question to ask. "Is anyone else in the village similarly stricken?"

Astrid took my hands as she answered. Two had come to her the night before, each under cover of darkness, having heard about Ylva's ailment. They'd been eager to know in what ways Astrid had attempted treatment. Neither had admitted to their children suffering but she had known, from their faces, that they carried the same burden.

My mind raced ahead, wondering how many might be keeping their condition hidden, even from those closest to them. These were my people now, and I would do whatever I could to rid them of this anguish.

4

The next morning, I mixed a salve of equal parts hazel bark and comfrey leaves, smoothed to a paste with honey.

Astrid was waiting for me at her door and her distress was clear. She hurried me inside, leading me to where Ylva sat trembling in her under-tunic. Her eyes appeared huge in her pale face.

I saw at once the cause of Astrid's fear. A red welt was rising on Ylva's cheek.

Astrid wrung her hands. "There's another on her back."

The baby grumbled in the corner, but Astrid made no move to comfort it.

I lifted Ylva's clothing to reveal the oldest sore: angry red on her shoulder, the skin broken at the edges, oozing yellow pus. The ones upon her neck were little better.

I wasted no time in applying the remedy, smoothing it upon the broken skin with a wooden spatula. "Twice a day, apply a small amount. Tie a strap of linen over the top to keep the poultice in place." I'd brought several strips of cloth with me, which I laid on the side, beside the pot of salve.

I gave Ylva a smile. "We'll have you better soon. Be brave."

In truth, the rapid spread of these sores made me anxious.

The fields were abundant in plants and herbs with curative powers, and I'd begun cultivating my own, on the sheltered side of the longhouse. However, the virulence of her affliction persuaded me that she needed a stronger remedy.

I'd always found that the most potent plants grew in the forest. Secreted in a leather pouch, I still had the Death's Cap I'd picked long ago and kept: its poison a talisman for my safety. I might have used it in those first days of the arrival of Eirik's men, when they'd plundered our village. I might have killed them all, had I wished to do so.

Some sense of humanity had stayed my hand. My role was to heal, not to harm.

Yet, I'd kept that deadly mushroom.

I'd ask Asta if I might accompany Helka into the woodlands, it being her custom to go hunting. She'd guide me deeper than I'd be able to venture alone.

I bid Ylva farewell, and Astrid walked me outside. I was reluctant to leave, knowing the troubles she bore.

"Avoid touching them, and keep them covered," I urged. "I'll visit again soon."

She nodded. I sensed there was much she wished to say, but there was no need. We understood each other.

"If anyone else wants my help, I'll be ready." I felt sure that Ylva was not alone. Behind closed doors, there would be others who fretted and feared.

Looking over her shoulder, I saw a woman standing no more than twenty steps away, watching with a ferocious expression. She carried a sturdy baby on her hip, fair-haired and with eyes of the lightest blue.

The woman's plait, falling over one shoulder, was a rich auburn-red. Even from a distance, I could tell the child was a boy, his features being pronounced in the way they rarely are among girl-children. He looked back at me earnestly, chewing upon something clutched in his fist.

"Who's that?" I asked Astrid. "Do you think she suffers as Ylva does?"

Astrid turned to look but spun back swiftly, moving her body to block the woman from my sight.

"It's Bodil, married to Haldor. Her oldest son was among Eirik's men when they went *a-viking*. It was his first trip across the sea. Like my husband, he did not return."

I felt a pang of sadness on Bodil's behalf. No wonder she regarded me with such a damnable glare. In her mind, her son's death had been at the hand of my former people.

I looked again at the child. In his face, there was something familiar to me. "That little one; he's a handsome boy."

Astrid's eyes skirted away. "He might be Haldor's… or he might not."

I could see for sure now. Those eyes were unmistakable, as was the bold set of the chin.

"Her husband knew, I think, but perhaps not." Astrid went on. "She weaves and sews well. There was a time when she was often at the longhouse, making clothes for Gunnolf and Asta."

"And for Eirik, too?"

Astrid's eyes told me all.

I kept to the other side of the way as I hurried past but, try as I might, I couldn't avoid the burning of her gaze. As I drew level, she spat fiercely upon the ground.

When Eirik took me in his arms that night, I thought of Bodil. Had she lain in this very bed? Had Eirik's weight pressed above her as he shuddered his release?

I imagined the imprint of her kisses, of her hands that had stroked and explored his body.

She must have looked for his longship even more eagerly than the others—anxious for the return of her lover. What jealousies she must feel.

I wondered with what words Eirik had parted from her and whether he'd been to visit her since his homecoming. It would be too cruel for him to allow her to discover by word of mouth that I'd taken her place.

And what of the child? Did Eirik know him for his own?

All these weeks I'd waited to feel his seed growing in me. I'd surrendered to his love-making countless times, but where was my baby?

My heart ached as he clasped me to him, telling me sweet things: I was his love, his enchantress, more precious than silver or gold, my beauty surpassing all other treasures. I shivered under his touch and cried as I rode the waves of my ecstasy.

I wished there to be no past, for either of us.

It would do me no good to think of Bodil or the other women who must have welcomed Eirik's embrace. How many followed me with ill-thoughts, borne of resentful rivalry?

I kept silent. To speak of my fears would be to make them real.

It was late into the night when I woke to a cool draught upon my skin and a figure looming above. I thought at first that it was Bodil, come to claim Eirik for her own and to pull me from the bed. In my half-wakened state, I saw her as some malevolent wraith.

Only when the figure spoke did I realize that another stood there: one who'd shared Eirik's bed perhaps more recently than Bodil.

"I'm here for him," Faline said. "If he wishes it."

My anger overtook any fear. "Eirik is asleep, as you can see." I reached for the covers, which she'd thrown from me as I slept. "Go back to your own bed. You aren't needed here."

"Another time." She gave no apology. If anything, I sensed her amusement.

How long had she stood over me?

5

The next day, as Helka and I set out, it reminded me of the first days of our acquaintance, when I'd led her into my own woodlands. My heart quickened as we left the bright sun of the open sky, entering the half-light of the forest. The season was turning but only a few trees had begun to alter their hue. Far above, the wind shimmered a lush canopy.

It had been some time since Helka and I had been alone, and I was gladdened to have her to myself. We walked briskly, Helka directing me to where dark sloes ripened on the bushes and the densest clutches of hazelnuts grew, for roasting.

It was upon the tip of my tongue to tell her of my meeting with Astrid. Helka was wise, and compassionate. However, some instinct guided me to keep the events of the previous day to myself. I'd tell her, perhaps, when I'd affected a cure. It would bring me greater pleasure to detail the challenge and my solving of it within the same story.

Of Bodil, I resolved to make no mention, for I wished to hear no confirmation of what pained me.

Our sacks were soon brimming with docks, nettles and lambs-quarters, milk thistle, figwort and heart of the earth.

I'd always felt most content in the forest. It was where I'd been free to climb and muddy my clothes, once upon a time. With the boys as my playmates, I'd learnt to be brave. My grandmother had indulged me until I began the path to womanhood. With that change, my liberty had ended. I'd cursed the day my aunt had followed my mother to the grave and left me to take her place in our chieftain's bed.

"You've become quiet, Elswyth." Helka placed a handful of lingonberries into her basket. "Does ought ail you?"

I popped a berry in my mouth, wincing at the bittersweet taste on my tongue. "Just remembering."

"You miss your village?"

I watched her fingers pluck the crimson fruit. "Only my grandmother. Not much else."

"And how do you settle?" she asked.

I gave a small shrug. "I don't yet belong, but I'll find my own way to be accepted."

"And Eirik is good to you?"

I nodded, squeezing a berry so that its juice ran over my fingers.

"As it should be." Helka smiled. "I see that you make him happy." She hesitated before continuing. "You know that others have shared his bed."

My chest tightened. Of course, I was aware, especially after my recent encounter with Bodil. It had been plain, too, from our first meeting—when Eirik had carried me over his shoulder into the Great Hall of my husband and had taunted me before his men. I'd thought he would strip and display me for all to see. Instead, he'd chosen another way—taking me to the chamber I'd shared with my husband until that morning, his blood still staining the floor.

"Among the thralls, there are few he hasn't bedded, but there are others too… though their husbands may not perceive it," Helka went on.

Thinking of the child upon Bodil's hip and how Bodil had looked at me with such malice, I knew perhaps more than Helka realized.

It wondered at the purpose of Helka's conversation. She did not usually speak in this rambling fashion. Indicating a fallen trunk nearby, she brushed away damp leaves and invited me to sit.

"I see that you wish to be more than Eirik's bed companion." She turned to look at me. "You wish to be his only one, his wife."

I plucked at some soft moss growing on the rotting wood and sat quietly. As the weeks had passed, I'd become aware of my deepening feelings for Eirik. I saw him not as my master, nor captor, but as the husband that I yearned for—the man I wished to father my children. I fell asleep with the smell of him and woke to the pleasure of his kisses, and the insistence of his morning desire.

I'd agreed to accompany Eirik to Svolvaen without promise of marriage.

I'd asked for nothing beyond what he'd already given me.

Nevertheless, it was true; I did want more.

"None has kept his interest as you do, but I say this to prepare you, Elswyth." Helka touched my arm. "It may never be."

As kindly as she meant the words, my heart gave a bruised leap. The wind rose at that moment and sent a wave through the branches, rippling the leaves, making it seem that they breathed with rustling sighs.

"His marriage is long overdue and, when it's made, it should be to a woman who brings not only a dowry but the promise of alliance. Svolvaen is prosperous, but we must grow stronger. As the ruling family, it's our duty."

I thought of Asta's arranged betrothal to Gunnolf. Was there already a woman promised to Eirik? My stomach churned at the thought.

Helka drew me closer. "I see that you understand and that it hurts you. Put your feelings aside, Elswyth. He will let you go when the time comes, but he will behave honorably. You're strong and will endure."

It seemed to grow quieter, as if the trees had pressed closer and were listening to us.

"When the time comes, you may continue serving Asta, keeping Eirik's bed when he desires it; or he'll find another man to be your husband."

Helka's face was all concern. I could see that she took no joy in telling me this. Nevertheless, a surge of anger took hold of me. "And what of you, Helka? Where is your alliance? Your husband is gone, and you have no children. Where is your marriage of duty?"

Her expression grew cold, and she drew back as if I'd attempted to strike her. At once, I regretted my sharp tongue. I knew well enough that she mourned Vigrid, though he'd died a full two years before.

I reached for her, wishing to put right my unkindness, but Helka stood and moved several steps away, presenting her back to me.

My eyes pricked. "Forgive me," I begged.

My disappointment had made me cruel, and I was ashamed. She spoke, I knew, only to warn me—to protect my heart.

It was some moments before she turned again. Her lashes were wet but there was steel in her voice. "You say this because you don't know…"

I was suddenly small and out of place, sitting among the dark ferns and twining roots. It had grown colder, and I felt myself an unwelcome intrusion in this ancient place. These were not the oaks and elms of my childhood forest. Their shadows fell differently. Even the far-off birdcalls seemed strange to me.

Helka gave a rueful smile. "Vigrid is gone, yet he lies beside me at night. I sense him though I cannot see him." She looked at me directly. "How, then, can I bring another into my bed?"

I knew not what to say. Though I'd seen my husband murdered in front of me, I hadn't grieved for him. I'd given him little thought since leaving my village. Helka's devotion was altogether different —more akin to mine for Eirik. Should I lose him, I would lose part of myself.

"It's only a feeling..." Helka wiped her sleeve to her face. "There are many things that may be felt, though they pass unseen."

"There's no... malevolence?" I asked, suddenly fearful. If my dead husband's spirit were to return to me, it would be in revenge or anger, not for love.

She shook her head. "I'm in no danger."

We walked on without speaking for a while, neither of us wishing to return to the subject and, at last, Helka advised that we turn back. The autumn was fully upon us, and the light fading earlier each day.

I agreed, but we had gone only a few steps when I noticed funghi growing upon a stump. I beckoned Helka for the use of her knife in collecting them.

Whether it was the ghost of our former conversation that lingered or something else that made her speak, Helka became serious again. "Elswyth, you feel an affinity with the forest, I know, but I must warn you not to venture too deeply, and never on your own."

Nearby, an owl hooted, and I thought of the wild creatures that must live here—bears and boar. I knew there to be stag and wolves. Helka had brought her crossbow, though we'd come across nothing larger than a rabbit.

Helka took my arm, urging me to keep walking. "There are parts of the forest in which I would never wander for fear of what I might find."

"Or what may find you." I gave a half-smile, wishing to show I was unafraid, but her manner sent a shiver through me.

Helka lowered her voice. "It's said that there are mysterious lights in the forest; lights that will lure you to danger."

My own people had a similar tale, but I'd never seen anything in our woods to frighten me. I'd hidden between the shadows of trees since I was very little.

"I don't believe in such things," I said firmly.

"Whether we believe them or not doesn't mean they may not be true." Helka pulled her cloak tighter. "Our people have passed down stories through the generations, and the *skalds* tell them to those who will listen, as they travel from place to place. They tell of deeds brave and foolish, and the downfall of those who think themselves invulnerable."

She continued to hurry me onwards, and before long, we saw the forest's edge. Helka indicated for us to put down our sacks and baskets and rest. The pale daylight was within sight, and the strange terrors that had risen up now receded.

"There is something else I wish to say before we return," said Helka. "Among the things which live in the forest is a seductive, secretive creature. She hides her true nature, to lure men. She shows only what is beautiful and enticing. She is the *huldra*: deceptive and vengeful."

"Many women must be part *huldra*, then," I added wryly.

"Does this creature not remind you of someone?" asked Helka. "There is something in Faline I cannot trust. I wish she were not under our roof."

I couldn't deny that I'd often thought the same myself. Yet, for some reason, I found myself unwilling to condemn her. After all, she was only looking after her own interests. I couldn't blame her for that.

She'd been the daughter of our chieftain. How different her life might have been had her promised betrothed not fallen from his horse. It seemed so long ago that I'd been married and suffered violence at my husband's hand.

In Eirik, I'd found someone to give my love to, and I received love in return, even if I were not his wife.

To my knowledge, there were none who gave Faline the same tenderness or affection.

I remembered, as a child, her asking to join us in our play. We'd found a tree which enabled us to climb higher than ever we'd climbed before. The boys laughed at her, so small she barely reached their waists, and told her to go home to her father. Had I mocked her, too, and sent her, tearful, back to the village? Perhaps I had.

Helka picked up her basket once more. "It was a mistake to bring her."

6

S ylvi watched as I crushed valerian root in the mortar with
petals of chamomile, cowslip and vervain I'd collected from
the meadow. I steeped the mixture in hot water to create a
draught.

"It's important not to use too much valerian," I warned, seeing
her interest. "Jarl Gunnolf only wants to sleep well through the
night, not fail to wake up altogether."

She nodded her understanding. If Sylvi ever wanted revenge on
the jarl for the liberties he'd taken with her, I'd shown her the way.
I hoped I wouldn't regret it.

Eirik needed no such help in sleeping, being tired from long
days stacking hay. The harvest was drawing to its end. The fields
were dusty yellow and scattered with broken straw, the fruit trees
stripped almost bare. The weather looked set to turn. The winter
fodder for our livestock had to be harvested before it began to rot,
then stored safely in the barns.

After we'd eaten the evening *nattmal*—a thick stew of mutton
and root vegetables served with bread and mead—Lady Asta took
her bath in the main hall of the longhouse, discreetly behind a

folding screen. Faline ladled steaming water into the tub from the cauldron over the firepit.

When I approached Gunnolf, he'd already begun to undress, having retired to the boxbed he shared with his lady. I did my best not to stare. His long hair, usually braided, hung loose about his shoulders.

He drank the sleeping draught down without hesitation, inclining his head in thanks. As I took the cup from him, he extended his finger to stroke mine. It was the lightest of touches, but I jerked away.

His cool eyes surveyed me. "What a nervous creature you are."

He pulled off his remaining garment and cast it to the floor. Standing before me naked, his gaze was unrelenting, as if defying me to look away.

My boldness rose in the face of that challenge, and, with coolness, I inspected his body. Like Eirik, he wore ink on his skin. Some designs were familiar to me, while others I could not make out, for the hair across his chest was dense and dark. It curled down the hardness of his stomach, joining that of his groin. His manhood hung large, though not erect.

"If you wish to see my cock at full attention, you'll need to apply yourself with a warm hand... or mouth." He sat on the edge of the bed and opened his thighs in languid invitation. "Or sit upon it, if you prefer."

His arrogance repulsed me, but his body was not unattractive, and his mouth was full and sensuous. I knew what sort of lover he was to Guðrún and Sylvi; the pleasure was all his own—greedy and selfish. With Asta, I imagined him gentle and considerate.

Something told me that, with me, he would be different altogether. Vanity and pride would spur him to prove himself Eirik's equal. That knowledge sent a thrill through my core—not of lust exactly, but a feeling of power. While I was unattainable, I would fascinate him.

35

It was a dangerous way of thinking.

Eirik had told me that he'd shared women with his brother in the past, but I believed he'd think less favorably of it in this case.

More importantly, I had no desire to betray Lady Asta. She turned a blind eye to many things, I was sure, but I would not have my own actions become a source of pain to her.

It was with some relief that I saw Gunnolf pull back the goatskins, lowering himself under them. His taunting demeanor was gone, the lines about his mouth set hard.

I saw something I recognized—a certain heaviness of heart from the burdens he was obliged to bear. It wasn't my place to speak, but the question escaped my lips before I thought to rein it in. "You suffer with troubling dreams?"

His eyes narrowed.

It was impertinent of me. I was no more than a thrall in his eyes, to be commanded or mocked.

It was only Eirik's claim upon me that had, so far, deterred Gunnolf from treating me as he did the other women serving in his household.

"My dreams are no concern of yours." He rolled his head wearily upon the pillow. "Go fuck my brother, and leave me to my rest."

***

Eirik was waiting for me, already beneath the furs. A lamp burned on the shelf within his boxed chamber, revealing his upper chest in shadow and light.

He watched as I let drop my belt and unfastened the brooches at my shoulders. I stepped from each garment until I was naked. I liked to see his gaze upon my breasts and the roundness of my hips, down to the blonde hair of my place of pleasure.

Smiling lazily, Eirik pulled back the covers, revealing more of his body to me. His voice was low. "I need you, Elswyth."

He drew me to him, and I pressed close, hardness meeting softness. He kissed me deep, and my body responded. With my thigh over his, it required only the smallest shift of my hip for him to enter.

Slowly, he began, clasping me by the cheeks of my buttocks as he thrusted. His hand crept between them, encouraging me to open further, to allow him deeper passage.

I surrendered to his lovemaking, wishing to make him part of my own body. He was my master in strength, but we were equals in our hunger for one another.

"Elswyth," he murmured, trailing kisses down my neck. "My own sweet love."

Already, my breath was quickening. I arched against his rhythm, my fingers curling into his hair. It took but a few strokes before he grasped me hard, ceasing his movement to pulse a hot stream of seed. When he kissed me again, it was with tenderness.

"Was Thor watching us?" I teased.

"He's always watching. We give him something worth looking at."

Easing his cock from me, he rolled away, but I'd no intention of letting him sleep. Warmed by what he'd given me, I wanted more.

Straddling him, I rested my sex upon the root of his fading erection. I knew he liked to see me so, with my hair falling wanton and my breasts above him. He rested his hands on my waist as I rocked lightly. His lips parted, wetted by his tongue.

It was impossible that Eirik could desire another with this burning passion that we shared.

He would never forsake me for a marriage of convenience. I wouldn't believe it. And yet, I recalled Helka's warning to me.

I wished to hear some promise of Eirik's love, some proof of his depth of feeling. I stroked the hair upon his chest and caressed his nipples.

"You wish to stir me again, my Valkyrie."

I licked where I'd touched, letting my breasts brush him lightly. Between my legs, I felt the base of his shaft thicken.

"We shall always be like this?" Kissing his abdomen, I moved downwards, tasting the sweat of our coupling. "You would never send me from your bed?"

"Of course not," he murmured. "You please me better than any woman."

"You'll protect me, always; love me, always?" I enclosed his cock with my hand.

"Aye, I will."

I took my tongue lower and closed my lips over the head of his penis, sucking at the tender spot beneath the head of his burgeoning erection. I opened my mouth wide, taking Eirik deep, past my teeth, to the back of my jaw. When I drew back, I let my tongue work the length of him.

He gasped, opening his legs and grasping my hair. "Don't stop!"

I sucked upon him again, drawing forth his brine. He was watching my mouth moving on him, my tongue licking at the fluid that trickled from his tip.

"I want the taste of you, Eirik."

He groaned as I took his balls into my mouth, humming so that he'd feel the vibration. I wanted him to know how delicious I found him.

At full arousal, it was more difficult to take him wholly in my mouth, but I returned to suck his length until I felt his tremor begin to rise. Swiftly, I diverted him into the warmth of my sex; only just in time, for he cried out and pulsed inside me.

When I blew out the lamp, I lay my head upon his chest. "You love me, Eirik?" I ran my fingertips over the raised scar down his side, a wound from long ago.

"Aye, I love thee."

He wrapped his arm about my shoulders, and I felt safe. He was mine and I was his.

"Forever?" I whispered.

In answer, there was only the soft, regular breathing of a man who had succumbed to sleep.

An old dream returned. I was circled by a beast. Despite my fear, I did not scream or run. Instead, I bared my breast to its claws. I watched as they peeled back the skin to reveal my beating heart. It lowered its shaggy head, licking the pulsing blood from my body.

7

L ate the next morning, I visited Astrid.

I half-expected Bodil to be waiting, to block my path and lay vengeful hands upon me, so far had my imagination built upon my previous meeting with her. Though I passed several of my new kinsmen, I was relieved to see that she was not among them.

In truth, Svolvaen seemed extraordinarily quiet. The weather was turning cooler, the sky overcast, but fine enough yet to work outside and make the most of the good daylight. However, the street lacked its usual bustle.

Eirik had been pleased to close the doors on the barn, knowing the winter fodder was safely stored. He'd gone out with the fishermen soon after dawn, eager for the smell of the sea. The fields had claimed too much of his time.

The stacking of the hay had brought the harvest to its close and some of the older men sat in leisure, taking a pipe and a horn of ale. They paused in their conversation as I passed, nodding their recognition, which I returned in kind.

It was a simple gesture but it warmed me, and I was emboldened to address a woman seated nearby. She'd been following my progress down the hill but glanced away as I approached, to the embroidery in her lap.

"Good morrow." I wracked my memory for the right words with which to praise her needlework. Her fingers were nimble with the thread: a vivid red against white cloth.

"It's very fine," I settled upon, at last. "Your hands are clever."

She raised her head at that and thanked me.

"You've come to see Astrid?" she asked. "I saw her looking from her door, watching for you, perhaps."

Her face was kindly, but I only nodded. It wasn't for me to reveal why Astrid might be expecting me.

"You're a good girl." The woman turned back to her work. "Pay no heed to anyone who says differently; they're only wishing they were in your place."

I thought, wryly, that none really knew what it was like to be 'in my place' but her kind words touched me, since I'd had few enough from the women of Svolvaen.

Further down the street, two women were talking but stopped abruptly as I drew near, looking at me with ill-concealed distaste. I waved my hand in greeting but they turned away, retreating into the house without a backward glance.

It will take time, I reminded myself.

The kindly woman had been right about Astrid waiting for me. She appeared at my first knock.

"Thank the gods you've come." She'd been weeping, her eyes ringed red.

"What is it, Astrid?"

Ylva was sitting with her back to us, carding wool, her younger brother playing at her feet.

"It's been only two days. It's no worse, surely? You've been using the salve I gave you?"

As soon as Ylva turned, I understood her fear. What had been no more than a rising welt upon her daughter's cheek had begun to blister.

"Show your shoulder," Astrid directed her.

Ylva winced as she removed the soiled cloth, which pulled at her tender skin. Beneath, the wound oozed wet, the smell unwholesome.

"And those on your neck?" I asked.

"There's a throbbing in them." Ylva's eyes, the same delicate grey as her mother's, beseeched me.

"I've brought something stronger, today." I adopted more confidence than I felt.

Quickly, I threw the old strip of bandage into the fire. "Don't try to wash this. Better to use new cloth each time. If you need to, at the very least, boil the old ones in the hottest water, then hang them to dry."

I took a pot from my apron pocket and spread a thick layer of green unguent onto the sore. "It's elm bark and yarrow, mixed with sage. It should bring down the swelling and draw out the poison."

"Thank you," whispered Ylva.

I smiled but kept my voice firm. "Wash your hands before you change your dressing, and afterwards."

Astrid, too, was attempting to be cheerful. She watched me closely, asking about the making of the balm. Despite her valiant efforts, I could see her distress. When all was done, I squeezed Ylva's hand and bid her to be brave.

"Have you heard from the women who came to you before?" I asked Astrid. "Ylva can't be the only one suffering with this."

It occurred to me that it might be a reason for the relative hush of the street. How many families were harboring a secret?

"If they share our troubles, they haven't told me, but I feel sure you're right. If they return to unburden their hearts, I'll tell them of your treatment," said Astrid.

I nodded and set the new pot of salve upon the table. "Twice a day."

Astrid indicated for us to go outside. She closed the door behind her and drew me close, speaking in hushed tones.

"I did have visitors but not the sort you're thinking of." She worried at her lip. "Ylva was betrothed to be married but the parents of the boy have broken the contract."

"They know?" It was a redundant question. Of course, they knew.

"Yesterday, when Ylva was shutting in the chickens, the boy came to her. She knew to keep her face well-hidden, but you know how young men are." Astrid gave a shuddering sigh. "He pulled off her scarf to kiss her and saw her cheek."

I imagined the whole of Svolvaen would know by now.

Astrid pushed aside a falling tear. "I can hardly blame them, but I fear for Ylva. Even if we cure her of this, people have long memories."

My heart ached for the girl. No doubt, she thought herself in love. The breaking of her betrothal must seem the end of all that mattered.

I put my arms around Astrid's shoulders as she stifled a sob. I feared that if I failed to heal her daughter it would be the end of more than Ylva's hopes for marriage.

8

The harvest was among the best Svolvaen had ever seen. The mild spring had encouraged orchard blossoms, followed by a warm summer of ripening the barley. No matter how deep the snow, the cattle would have their fodder. We'd laid down pears and apples for the winter, between straw, and conserved plums in their own syrup, packed tightly in jars. Every house had its provision of smoked herring, root vegetables and honey, its own store of mead and of ale. No matter what storms came, Svolvaen wouldn't starve.

Now all had been gathered in, Jarl Gunnolf invited Svolvaen to join in a day of festivity. There was to be a contest of one-to-one combat, followed by falconry and then carousing, long into the night.

As people gathered outside the longhouse, I looked among the crowd for anyone wearing a cowl about their neck. It would be a sign, perhaps, of them wishing to cover the affliction I believed was travelling among them.

Astrid waved to me. She had her toddling son lifted in her arms, that he might better see. The baby, I supposed, she'd left with Ylva, at home.

The jarl wore his customary black, including a cloak of dark brocade, trimmed thickly in silver fur. Beside him, his Lady was radiant in a gown of white, embroidered in gold and yellow. Asta rested her hands upon the growing babe within her, the swell of her belly visible. She smiled at her people, applauding each man who stepped forward to indicate his participation.

"The jarl will preside over pairs of men, in successive bouts," Helka explained, "Until only one remains."

Eirik waited until all others had presented before showing his own willingness. Stripped to the waist, with his hair fastened into a top knot, he stood taller than the rest. I'd seen him wield his axe, and had tended to him on return from battle, streaked with other men's blood, but had never witnessed him wrestle skin on skin.

"Odin and Thor and all the gods are among us!" Gunnolf announced, slitting the throat of a sturdy hog. There was a mighty cheer as a gush of crimson flooded at his feet. The animal would spend the rest of the day roasting, in readiness for the evening feast. "Just as this life-force soaks the soil, so doth ours, shed in combat. May our deeds always be brave and glorious, so that all may know of the greatness of Svolvaen."

As the tournament began, I saw that agility counted for as much as strength. Each took up the great horn of honeyed mead, drinking deeply before they commenced. Grappling within a designated square, no more than five steps wide, the first to pin their rival to the ground for the count of ten took the bout.

The shouts of those watching were deafening, roaring approval at each triumph. The outcome of some pairings was decided almost immediately. Others left their opponents staggering from exertion, sinews straining in pursuit of conquest.

Eirik seemed to win his matches with little effort, having not only skill in the various holds but the might to lift another man from his feet. Yet, none seemed to mind his ascendancy. He allowed each man a fair chance to demonstrate his prowess before asserting his own. Eirik helped them to stand tall, clasping his combatants about the shoulders in congratulation on a match well fought.

It was clear that he delighted in conquest as much as any man but valued fellowship above all, and these were his men, whom he had led across the seas, to return with riches and renown.

When the final bout was declared, Eirik faced his old friend, Olaf—both muddied from the many matches they'd already claimed. What Olaf lacked in stature, he made up for in lightness of foot, twisting repeatedly from Eirik's grasp, to the mirth of those watching. Eirik could have taken Olaf to the ground at any time but chose, instead, to revel in festive merriment, indulging Olaf's antics to avoid him.

Gunnolf followed closely, his eyes alight. Had Eirik been, at last, beaten, our jarl would have had trouble concealing his satisfaction, I thought. There was another too, whose eyes were all for Eirik. Bodil neither cheered nor clapped but watched with quiet intensity.

Was she recalling, I wondered, the sweat of their own bed-wrestling? Jealousy burned in my belly at that thought, for Eirik was mine.

At last, with an indomitable cry, Eirik subdued Olaf, holding him by ankle and wrist. As the count neared ten, Eirik gave his rival a playful tweak of the nose and pulled him to his feet.

The clamor was great indeed, with all shouting Eirik's name, and I saw a shadow pass over Gunnolf's face.

However, Eirik knelt before the jarl. "My victories or losses are in the hands of the gods. If I have strength, it is through their grace, and I offer it in your service. Send me where you will, upon any mission, and I will bring glory to your name and to that of Svolvaen."

It was a speech delivered from the heart and, once more, the men received Eirik with thunderous approval. It required the jarl's raised hand to gain the peace he needed to reply.

"I accept your service, which I know is given in good faith. May you be an example to all men, in your allegiance to your jarl." Gunnolf placed his own drinking cup in Eirik's hands, but I noted a tenseness in his jaw.

I didn't wish to see the day Gunnolf believed Eirik's loyalty to be in question.

The men lifted down trestle tables from the rafters of the great hall, for a midday repast of smoked ham and cheeses, fruit and flatbread. The ale flowed, bellies were full, and spirits were high.

As I helped in carrying jugs of mead, Eirik beckoned me to him.

"There are others to serve." Eirik placed his hand upon my waist. "Today, everyone should see the regard I have for you."

Never before had he accorded me such public recognition and it pleased me greatly.

I commended him on his performance, for it was as much that as a show of physical prowess.

"Aye, I won't deny it." He shared his smile with me. "There's little need for me to prove myself among my own men. They know my strength already."

"And what of Gunnolf's strength?" I sliced an apple. Its tang went well with the goats' cheese before us. "Does he fear it would be his face pushed in the dirt, were he to take part?"

Eirik looked at me askance.

"Bold talk for such a little mouse under the jarl's roof." He took a piece of apple from my plate. "We're different, he and I, but no man had a truer brother. He would give his life for me, as I would for him."

I lowered my eyes, choosing not to answer. As jarl, Gunnolf had authority, but I doubted he had the men's love as his younger brother did.

The meal being taken, horses were brought. Gunnolf mounted a dappled grey, that shook its white mane as he took his seat. Eirik's was a golden roan, solid of leg, with a deep barrel. There were perhaps twenty in all and Eirik led a chestnut mare for me to climb, with a blaze upon its nose. It was Asta's, though I'd never seen her on its back.

"You'd like to come?" he asked. "Join our hawking?"

I had not much experience of riding, but I took my seat without difficulty. I looked back, to see our Lady waving. She'd want to hear of the excitement, later, and I'd no wish to disappoint her.

Of course, Helka was among the riders.

"The men will race on, in pursuit of the birds," she told me. "Stay close. The best hunting will be in the fields south of the forest, but our ride may take us near the clifftops. There are fissures hidden in the grass. A wrong footstep and your sweet mare would break its leg or fall. Some chasms are large enough to take a horse whole, and the unfortunate rider."

I shuddered at the thought.

"You'll be safe with me," she promised. "Keep by my side."

Gunnolf unhooded his falcon, which clutched the leather of his cuffed arm. "Are you ready, brother?" His eyes were as wild and unfathomable as those of the dark-plumed peregrine.

I sensed at once that this contest would lack the mirth of the men's wrestling bouts.

"Aye, always," came Eirik's returning shout. He took his own bird, brought to him tethered on its leash. "Your hunter may be more powerful, but mine has been with me since she was a chick." He stroked its soft, speckled breast, looking into the hawk's amber gaze. "She's the better trained, I'll wager."

"And what do you wager?" Gunnolf called in return.

"Whatever you wish." Eirik grinned. "All that's mine is yours. I can deny you nothing."

"Spoken well, brother. I shall think on it…" With that, Gunnolf let fly his peregrine.

Eirik kissed the sleek head of his pretty hawk, before casting her to the wind.

The jarl gave his mount a swift kick and set off toward the woods, leaving the rest of us to follow.

With the wind in our faces, we skirted the trees then dropped down toward the open meadows and the straw-blown fields.

The birds soared and chased one another. The peregrine darted so close, at times, I thought it would wing Eirik's hawk, but they flew on, swift and agile.

Gunnolf's bird was the first to catch sight of prey, and he cried his delight to see it dive.

Helka and I had been to the rear of the party—my lack of skill keeping me from being as fleet as the others. We now drew alongside.

The peregrine sat upon its prize, tearing fur and flesh with its razor-beak before Gunnolf's sharp whistle summoned its return. The hare was limp, its eyes glassy in unexpected death. With a shake of feathers, the bird deposited the creature, resuming its place on its master's forearm.

"You've coddled your little hawk, brother." Gunnolf rewarded his own bird with a chunk of raw meat. "She seems not the mighty huntress you believe her to be."

Eirik held out his cuff, inviting his hawk to alight there.

"And what do you wish from me, my jarl?"

"Only the pleasure of an initiation."

Eirik bowed his head. Meanwhile, Gunnolf brought his horse close to mine.

I felt the heat of its flank, and my mare tossed her head away from the intruding muzzle of the dappled grey.

I'd never been so near to a falcon. It was a handsome creature, stately and graceful, but I felt myself shrink from its crimson-stained beak and its unblinking gaze.

One of the men threw the hare to Gunnolf, who caught it in his free hand and pressed his thumb to the wound. The blood bubbled from the jagged tear at its throat.

I felt a moment of panic, being unsure what Gunnolf intended. Whatever he required of me, I felt bound to comply. I could not break Eirik's promise without shaming him.

"You may skit as swiftly as the hare, but you can't escape." Speaking low enough that no other could hear, he daubed my forehead before dropping the pad of his thumb to my lower lip. The intimacy of it startled me. Instinctively, I licked the moisture away, finding it bitter upon my tongue.

"The first time is sweetest." Gunnolf's gaze lingered upon my lips.

I turned away, discomforted by this attention, but avoided looking at Eirik.

Tossing the hare away, Gunnolf raised his arm.

His soft whistle sent the peregrine back into the sky. Eirik then released his hawk, and the two took the breeze under their wings. Circling and swooping, lifting on the wild currents of the wind, the birds disappeared into the clouds.

We craned to see them and, at last, the hawk emerged with the other on its tail. It was a game of chase, it seemed. However, the falcon's pursuit was relentless. The smaller bird skittered low over the field while its rival hovered above. As the hawk struggled to rise, the peregrine seized its chance. It dived, rearing up its claws at the final moment, knocking the air from Eirik's huntress, sending it tumbling.

The bird hit the earth upon its back. It was unmoving but for the flutter of one wing. Eirik rode to the spot, dismounting to take the hawk in his arms.

It trembled briefly, then lay still.

9

I'd long ago put away the garments I'd brought with me, for they marked me as an outsider. Helka most often wore tunics and trousers but had given me some aprons, woven from flax and dyed in shades of russet and green. They suited me well enough; engraved bone brooches fastened the straps over each shoulder.

She berated me for lack of skill in weaving cloth. Even she, whose time was spent more in hunting, knew how to work a loom. Her fingers were nimble but, when I tried, everything tangled. It had always been so.

"You're too impatient, Elswyth," she chided, showing me how to use the heddle rods to separate the threads of warp. She passed the weft through on its shuttle. "You desire to have all you wish without applying yourself to the labor of the task. All things worthy of attaining require our constancy."

I knew myself well enough to see the truth of it. I'd always been inclined to impulse and hastiness. I wished for action, not the monotony of hours at the loom. My stitching was little better, whether my needle was bone or wood. I preferred the dyeing of the cloth, knowing well which leaves and tubers produced the brightest hues.

My one true skill was my knowledge of healing plants and herbs, but I still hadn't found a cure for the sores which plagued Ylva.

The salve I'd made from elm bark, with sage and yarrow, had curbed the spread of the poison, but the skin refused to heal. My treatment had prevented the blight on her cheek from becoming an open sore, but the skin remained red and swollen, the infection lingering beneath the surface. I feared to lance it as I would a boil.

Astrid told me that Ylva sobbed through the night, for the loss of her young man.

Not for the first time, I wished my grandmother were with me. I missed her company and her wise guidance. I wondered if she were already dead, and her home cleared of its simple possessions. If I returned, would I find some other family living there, in the home I'd once shared with her.

The weather was full of the north wind now, and the first snow flurries had come to Svolvaen.

"We'll soon be contained indoors. If the winter's hard, the harbor may even freeze over. We shouldn't waste this time," Helka urged. "Come. We'll go fishing."

Asta insisted that I take the opportunity. Her belly was growing fast but she still wished to attend herself in most matters. Faline would keep her company in my absence.

I'd not been upon the water since the great journey that had brought me to Svolvaen, and I was not a natural seawoman, but Helka assured me that I'd be safe in her care.

"Only move as I direct you," she commanded, "Or we'll find out how well you swim."

The air was fresh and the wind brisk, and I understood immediately why she liked to sail. There was an immense feeling of freedom, and it was beautiful, with the sunlight quivering on the water. She took us between the cliffs, and I gazed upwards, wondering at the height of the sheer rock.

"The men collect auk eggs in spring, climbing down from the top, attached to ropes," Helka told me.

The very thought of it made my head spin. It appeared too steep to climb. I could see no obvious footholds.

"You need a head for heights. It's not for everyone," Helka admitted.

"And you?"

"I prefer not to." She looked up at the whirling seabirds. A gannet dived not far off, emerging with a silver fish in its long beak. "The life of the chicks is precarious enough without us eating those eggs."

The tide was with us, taking us out towards the open sea, although the wind blew inland.

"The fishing boats go out in all but the worst weather. Mine too, although only as far as the mouth of the fjord. Beyond that, the waves are too strong." She patted the side proudly and pointed to the net folded at our feet. "You throw it out and let the wind take your sail, then pull it in afterwards."

"As easy as that?"

"You'll see." Helka nodded for me to take up the net. We fastened it to the rear of the boat before casting it a good distance behind. 'Now, we move the tiller and turn the boat, so the wind is behind us. Our net will swell out as we move through the water, and the fish will be trapped inside.'

We spent the next few hours sailing back and forth, letting the wind carry us, the net filling with four or five fish each time, until we had quite a haul.

When Helka turned us back, she took us close to the cliffs, so that I might peer into the caves. The opening of one was wider than the rest.

"I used to hide here when I was younger. There's a flat space, where it's possible to sit or lie down, and you can take a small boat right inside if you bring down the mast. You can tie it there, out of sight."

She steered us closer still, being careful to avoid the jagged rocks on either side of the entrance, where the waves splashed and split.

"Did you have cause to hide very often?"

"No more often than my brothers." Her lips twitched in a smile. "But not even Eirik knew where I went. It's good, sometimes, to have a secret place."

I conjured an image of the three of them as children, Helka playing with her brothers as I had with the boys of my own village. I thought back to Gunnolf's marking of me with blood from the hare. As a child, I imagined him hungry for ascendancy over his siblings. He would have thought it his due, as the oldest.

There was a rising in the wind, sending the gulls wheeling from the ledges above, to glide white upon the air.

"I had something similar," I mused. "Part of the woods where the other children didn't like to go, and a particular tree I'd climb. One of the branches was wide enough to curl upon. I stayed there all night once. I'd forgotten to shut in the chickens, and the fox came and killed all but two of them."

"You were punished?" asked Helka.

"My grandmother smacked me, and I ran away."

"And how long did you stay hidden?"

"Only until the next day. I came home ravenous and was given three bowls of soup, with another clout for making my grand-mother worry."

"Ah!" declared Helka. "I was better prepared. I used to keep food in the cave, in a leather bag, and a bottle of mead."

I raised my eyebrows. How wonderful it would've been to have known Helka when I was growing up.

"I was a clever girl, yes?" She smiled in satisfaction, and I nudged her playfully.

"I still store some things there. We never know what may come... and a hiding place can be useful." Her face was serious again. "Although I'm beginning to think I should stop running away from what frightens me."

Her thoughts were evidently no longer upon childish things, and I wondered what it was that Helka feared. She'd tell me, I supposed, when she had a mind to do so.

"If ever I need to hide, I'll come here."

"Except that I shall know where to find you." Helka smiled. "Not such a good hiding place!"

"But I shan't mind if you find me." I squeezed her arm. "I'll be waiting, knowing that you'll come and make everything all right again."

"Always, Elswyth, if it's in my power," Helka promised.

10

Winter's dark crept closer, until Svolvaen huddled snowbound. The world shrank to silence and the crunch of white underfoot. Thankfully, our provisions were stored and smoked and pickled. Our fires protected us from the frosted world beyond.

Gunnolf and Olaf spent many hours at a game in which counters moved about the board. I asked Helka to teach me, but she asserted it was a pastime for which she'd never had the patience. She paced more even than Eirik, lifting the skins at the small openings beneath the roof, a frustrated captive gazing through the ever-falling snow.

I visited Astrid when I could, each time adapting my salve, changing the proportions of my ingredients, adding a dash of something new. I'd dried plentiful amounts of what I found useful, to aid me in my remedies. Nevertheless, though I had arrested the spread of Ylva's sores, they refused to heal.

Feeling an itch over my skin, I'd wonder if the blight had come upon me. As the weeks passed, I thanked the gods, old and new, that my flesh remained unblemished.

It was a cold, clear night as I pushed through the wind to reach Astrid's hut. The snow had crusted hard. I was grateful for my goat-skin cloak to wrap about me, and my boots of rabbit fur, laced to the knee.

The harshness of the weather kept Svolvaen's residents inside their homes, and perhaps it was for the best. I remained convinced that others were afflicted but had no means of knowing to what extent.

As soon as I entered, I saw that my fears had not been unfounded. There were four others before Astrid's hearth: three children and their mother, each marked by the same sore as Ylva bore on her cheek. I wondered how many weeks their affliction had been festering, for the wounds glistened wet.

"Thank goodness you've come." Astrid left the cauldron she'd been stirring, helping me remove my cloak. "We've been hoping you'd make it out today."

"There's no need to explain. I can see why I'm needed." I returned Astrid's hug of welcome. "And Ylva?"

"She's much the same; no worse."

Ylva appeared from behind a curtain separating their latrine. Looking from her cheek to that of the woman by the fire, I saw how far my remedy had helped. Ylva's sore was red but gave no discharge.

"The others: on your shoulder and neck, on your back?"

Ylva lowered her eyes, uncomfortable to speak of them. "They still trouble me, but the salve is soothing; it helps—at least for a time."

"This is Torhilde." Astrid introduced the woman by the fire.

I nodded, giving her and the little ones a smile of encouragement. "You did the right thing, coming here."

Her eyes had a feverish brightness to them, but also a look of despair. "My husband won't have us under his roof." She pulled the smallest child onto her lap. "Not like this."

I placed my hand on her forehead and felt heat there. The children were listless, their skin clammy.

"They can stay here, of course," said Astrid. "When they're better, he'll have them back." She rested her hand upon the woman's shoulder.

I bit back what I wanted to say: that no man who abandoned his wife and children in illness deserved to have them return. It was not for me to judge how others lived, and I had no marriage of my own to hold as an example.

Despite my doubts about her husband, I sought to reassure her. "I'm sure he only fears contagion. If he were to fall ill, it would serve no purpose."

I concentrated on the matter in hand. "Astrid, you remember what we did before, for Ylva?"

She nodded. "I've the hot water ready and put comfrey leaves in to steep."

We set about cleaning each sore upon the children's bodies, applying the salve I'd brought with me for Ylva. It pained me to see the ugly marks which tainted their young skin, but I comforted myself that they'd soon have some ease. We undressed Torhilde last, and I was horrified. Seeing the extent of her suffering, it surprised me less that her husband had turned her from their home.

At last, all was done, and I promised to soon return. Knowing Astrid couldn't feed so many without depriving herself, I resolved to bring some jars from our own store. It seemed to me that the longhouse was provisioned to endure three winters; none would miss what I took.

I headed back, into the night, to those who awaited my return.

"Sing for us, my love."

I entered to see Gunnolf placing Asta's lute in her arms. He lifted her hair back from her shoulders, that her fingers might find the strings of the instrument more easily.

"What would you have me play?" she asked, her eyes lit by his touch. "I fear you know all by heart."

"Whatever pleases you, wife." Gunnolf dropped a kiss upon her forehead, before laying on the furs about the firepit.

Despite these gestures of affection, his gaze strayed towards me as I joined them. I paid no heed, but I was sure Faline caught his look. I hoped only that Asta did not notice such things.

We ate well and the flames blazed. It was easier to bear the incessant moaning of the wind when we were comfortable inside. I closed my eyes and lay back my head upon Eirik's chest. We were a small gathering that night—only Helka and Olaf being with us.

I'd thought Asta would choose a love ballad. Instead, her voice filled the great space of the longhouse with an ominous tale, of the long winter coming, when all would freeze and wither. Her haunting melody told of the doom of the gods and the horror which would overwhelm the world. The great wolf Fenrir would break its bonds and its jaws would ravage, until even the sun was dragged into the beast's belly. With the beast's last howl, the land would sink beneath the sea, into perfect silence.

We neither moved nor spoke as Asta's melancholy song rang out those dark prophecies of Ragnarök, but it seemed a shadow moved through the room, touching each one of us.

The last notes of the lute left us with the moan of the night wind beyond the safety of our walls, and we took our forebodings to our beds.

11

For so long, I'd slept against the warmth of Eirik's body and woken to his heated passion. My need was as great as his and not just by night. Eirik sought me out in whatever task I was engaged. Wrapping his arms about my waist, he melted me with his kisses, his mouth hot upon my neck, before carrying me to his bed.

I watched and waited for my belly to grow, desiring motherhood as I never had with the husband I had not loved—the husband Eirik's men had slaughtered. I remembered creeping from my bed as he snored, washing him from me to avoid a baby coming.

Eirik seemed blind to Faline's seductive glances. In this, and in his constant yearning for the comfort of my body, I saw love.

Helka ate with us most days, though she sometimes preferred her own company, retreating to the home she'd shared with her husband, Vigrid. Asta, meanwhile, slept a great deal.

Eirik would sit by the fire with Olaf and Gunnolf and several of the other men. One evening, as I undressed for bed, I listened to their voices, raised in laughter—these Northmen who fought at one another's side. They were recalling some battle and their various braveries. It was the sort of talk Eirik loved, but he would soon come to me, I knew.

Lying naked upon the furs, my bare skin tantalized by their softness, I stroked between my legs. Dipping into the growing wet, I thought of Eirik's vigor, the hardness of his body and his warrior strength.

His weapons filled the outer portion of our chamber: an iron-headed spear, a light crossbow, feathered arrows as long as my arm, the helmet of leather and steel that fitted smooth to Eirik's head, and his chainmail tunic. His sword, wrought from twisted steel and iron, hammered into an unyielding edge, stood unsheathed. Even in the dim light it gleamed, as if with its own vitality, remembering the many limbs it had severed and the crimson libations it had claimed. Heart of the Slain he called it, for its power over life and death.

When Eirik pulled back the curtain, he smiled to see me ready, my fingers starting what I wished him to continue.

I teased him with a view of what lay inside me.

Grasping my waist, he pulled me to the edge of the bed. "Full of sweetness," he murmured.

He lowered to taste me, and I shivered as he delved deeper. He pressed the point of his tongue where I most desired it, then pulled me more firmly onto his mouth, devouring my softness.

I squirmed beneath him, upon the very edge of my ecstasy, and did not curb my mewling pleasure. I was not ashamed of the noises I made. It excited me, even, to think of others listening, hearing the satisfaction of our bedding.

"Oh, my sweet one." Freeing himself, Eirik swiftly guided his shaft, delivering his full length into my yielding flesh. I panted with the force of his thrusts, lifting my hips to meet him until my voice gave its final rising.

Eirik groaned and clenched, holding himself deep. There was a cheer and laughter from the adjoining room, at which Eirik grinned, collapsing beside me.

"You would never share me, would you, Eirik? I'm yours alone." It was a question which still preyed upon my mind.

"Nay, I would not." Eirik nuzzled my shoulder. "Though any man watching you writhe beneath me would want his share. You are my woman, Elswyth. No other shall have you."

His answer pleased me, and we made love again—slowly this time, rocking languorously until the end, and with Eirik's kisses gentle on my lips.

I dozed, and all was quiet through the night, but some sound stirred me: a crying out. I placed my tunic over my head, then looked into the great space of the hall.

The embers of the fire pit were glowing still. From the far end, where Asta slept, came a low keening.

As I hurried through, I saw Guðrún peeking from the alcove in which we prepared food, with Sylvi behind her.

Another curtain, which concealed where Faline slept, swept aside. Gunnolf appeared, bare-chested. Faline was beside him, her fingers curled about his arm.

He inclined his head to me—in recognition, I supposed, for my having risen to attend his wife. My returning nod was brief before I looked away.

The lamp's wick was lit on her bedside, its illumination showing me the paleness of her face. She sat up in the bed, her eyes not her own—so wild and dark. I wrapped her close, for she trembled.

"Did you hear him?" She clung to me, her cheek clammy against mine.

I thought she referred to Gunnolf and his wayward behaviour. It was a subject none mentioned in Asta's presence.

"Nay, my Lady. I heard nothing. The house is quiet." I rocked her gently upon my shoulder.

"I couldn't find him, no matter how I looked."

"Only a bad dream," I soothed, encouraging her to lie back.

"Where do they go? The babies that die?" She licked her lips and I saw they'd grown cracked.

"Your child is well, growing safe inside you." I smoothed a tendril of hair from her forehead. "There's nothing to fear."

She cradled the curve of her belly. "I couldn't watch when they put him in the fire. The smoke carries them to the next world; that's what they say, but I don't know if I believe it."

"We all have dark thoughts, but no one will harm your baby. I'll make sure of that." Taking her hand in both of mine, I whispered softly, saying whatever I could to pacify her. "You've had a nightmare. It's no more than dream-nonsense."

In her fright, she looked more like a child than a grown woman and I was reminded that she was little more than my own age.

I attempted to rise, but she wouldn't release my hand. "Gunnolf promised not to burn my body; he'll bury me where we put the ashes."

"Ashes?"

"From my first." Asta lifted herself from the pillow, pulling me closer. "He's alone, under the frost, in the forest."

In all the months I'd tended her, she'd never mentioned another birth. What pain there must be, to bind bones and flesh and to be aware of the heartbeat of another, only to see that creation brought to nothing. It was little wonder her mind strayed to this lost child, but it would do no good to dwell on what was gone.

"We can't choose our time of death," Asta asserted, her voice faint, yet resolved. "Only the Nornar may do that."

I remembered Helka telling me of this legend: that the three women of destiny carved each life upon a stave of wood at the time of our entering the world. It was this that inspired the bravery of the Norsemen, Helka said, for what is there to lose when a man's fate is predestined.

"It's like *The Song of Skirnir*." Asta gripped my hand. "My life is fashioned down to the last half-day."

"No more of that, my Lady. Think of the new baby coming. How happy you'll be then."

The tension seemed to leave her body and she released my fingers.

"I think I shall never see it." She spoke quietly but I heard every word.

An unsettling feeling overtook me as we sat there, wrapped in shadows. Looking at her face so pale, I saw the skull beneath her skin, and shuddered.

12

Winter continued, in snow-deep slumbering stillness. As the very darkest days approached and the festival of *Jul* drew near, some ventured forth with the full moon to gather mistletoe. The same scythes that had reaped maize and barley from the fields brought down the evergreen foliage, rich in white berries, dangling in great clusters from the trees.

I tied the bunches tight, passing them to Helka, who climbed on Eirik's shoulders to hang them from the rafters. Steadying herself against the great beam of wood above her head, her fingers worked nimbly to secure the thread. "The god of light, Baldur, was slain by an arrow of mistletoe and was sent to reside in the cold and misty Underworld, in everlasting night. The goddess Hel kept him, though he was a reluctant consort."

"And did he stay there for ever more?" I never tired of hearing these stories, though they didn't always make sense to me.

"Nothing lasts forever. It's said that he'll return when Ragnarök ends, and the cycle of life begins again. From death, he'll be reborn. Until then, he must endure, as we do, through winter's grip on the frozen Earth."

"On the first night of *Jul*, when the daylight is shortest, we keep vigil until dawn," said Eirik. "No matter how fast Sól drives her chariot, fleeing Fenrir, the devouring wolf of darkness, she's doomed to be swallowed by his ravening jaws. We must wait and watch, to show our need for her to rise again."

There had been a time, long ago, when I'd hidden up a tree to escape a wolf. I remembered the saliva upon its fangs and the steady gaze of its pale eyes. Wolves were beautiful creatures but unpredictable, and always hungry. They were not to be trusted.

Helka reached down as I passed along more mistletoe.

"It's the night of Odin's Wild Hunt," went on Eirik, "When he leads the immortal souls of our ancestors, charging across the sky on Sleipnir, his eight-legged stallion."

The thought filled me with awe. "Have you seen this, Eirik?"

"No wise man ever has." Eirik moved a few steps so that his sister could reach further along the beam. "It would be too dangerous to meet the Ásgardr riders. The border between the worlds of living and dead is not always fast, especially when these winter days make the Earth resemble the dark and cold of Hel's merciless Underworld."

"We leave gifts of food and drink in the snow," Helka added. "So that they pass on without danger."

I'd been raised a Christian and knew my own people would be preparing to honour the day of the Saviour's birth. However, we had older stories not unlike these—of winter's darkness and the light that would come again. We decorated our homes with wreaths of green and mistletoe through the months of frost to remind ourselves of the waiting Spring. We had, too, our rituals to deter the eye of mischievous spirits that roamed most freely when the Earth became a wild and inhospitable place for man.

Helka's stories spoke to my blood, and I sensed the truth of them.

With her foot, she nudged Eirik's shoulder to return her to the ground. He gave me a wink then made a purposeful wobble, pretending to drop his sister, for which she rewarded him with a clip to his ear.

"Have no fear, Elswyth." Regaining her feet upon the ground, Helka looked up to admire her handiwork. "The forces of the restless dead have no reason to harangue you."

"Indeed, not," I answered, but I thought of my husband, whom I'd never mourned, and of my grandmother, left behind across the sea. Had she passed into the next world? I had no way of knowing.

The men dug through the snow to allow passage up the hill, and the longhouse was soon filled with ribald laughter and boisterous sports. Torhilde was absent but Ylva came with her mother, though she kept to the corner of the room and wore her cowl close. The blight upon her cheek was hardly visible in the dim light but I knew she would be conscious of its marking.

Eirik brought me a new gown to wear, in a becoming shade of violet blue, its bodice embroidered with pansies.

"Wear your golden hair loose, today, as Asta does." He placed a kiss upon my neck. His own tunic was of the same cloth, embroidered with sheaves of barley at the hem.

Gunnolf donned the skin and head of a goat, sacrificing four of the sturdy animals and a pig for the three-day banquet that was to begin. Several women helped Guðrún and Sylvi prepare the victuals. I understood, then, why our pantry had been stocked so full.

My mouth watered over the abundant pots of stew and the richly scented roasting meat. Eirik cut a slice from the pig's shoulder and fed it to me, hot and running thick with juices.

A huge log of oak burned beneath the spit, with holly sprigs and fir branches thrown atop.

"Rake through the ashes in the morning and save the largest

pieces," Asta told me. "We'll hang them up to bring good fortune for the coming year."

Before closing the great doors, they rolled out a giant wheel, carved from wood kept dry in the barn. Gunnolf set it aflame, and Olaf and Eirik pushed it off. It whirled down the hill—a burning symbol of the sun, cutting through the darkness—its journey ending somewhere in the meadow.

It wasn't long before the drinking games began, the men competing against the women. The jarl and his lady sat in judgment, deciding which rhymes and insults were most filled with wit. It was no surprise that Helka shone in weaving puns and riddles. She easily gained the better of the men who challenged her. Eirik soon held up his hands and surrendered before his sister. Lifting her onto his shoulders as he'd done when they'd hung the mistletoe, he paraded her about the room as the victor in their battle.

It was good to see her laughing, and Astrid, too. In that atmosphere of merrymaking, the women linked me into their arms, united in sharing their drollery at the expense of their menfolk. My heart swelled with a new feeling of acceptance. More than ever, I was glad to have made my journey to join Eirik, to begin this new life.

A tug of war followed, wives pitted against husbands, with the children watching wide-eyed as their mothers planted their feet and pulled with all their might. The women of Svolvaen were strong of arm, and the contest was a close one, though it ended with skirts flying, as they were brought to the ground by the superior brawn of their men.

"Come now, mothers, sisters and daughters," declared Asta. "In gracious forfeit, refill their cups and embrace these men beloved. Rejoice that their strength in sport is also the strength that protects us in times of battle."

Eirik was the recipient of more kisses than seemed his due, but

I was content to let him revel in them. It was a night of festivity after all. It was well into the night before people nodded to sleep upon the benches ranged each side of the great hall, sleeping off the mead they'd enjoyed.

The dawn was thin and grey, but I smiled to see it. If Odin's terrible hunt had passed over our roof, I'd heard nothing. Through the second day of feasting, we listened to tales of man-eating trolls, giants, and the gods—their cleverness and trickery, jealousy and deceits. I laughed at how Odin dressed as a bride to retrieve his powerful hammer, and shivered to hear Helka tell the full story of sweet Baldur's sojourn in the hidden world of the dead. There was much drinking and eating, the women sharing their gossip as they prepared the table.

Later, Gunnolf encouraged the men in games of chance and threw down a challenge.

"Your hand, brother," he proclaimed, resting his elbow upon the table, "And we shall test your prowess." Filled already to the brim with ale, he slurred his words.

Eirik was no better, and the result was part comical, as each vowed to prove the superiority of their arm. Yet, there was an edge to the jarl's sport. With sleeves pushed to their elbows, it was clear that the contest was in earnest, at least on Gunnolf's part. His teeth clenched in grim determination as they pushed back and forth. Bringing Eirik's fist to the wood, Gunnolf gave a shout of triumph and there was a wildness in his eyes.

While his men cheered his conquest, I thought their hails lacked the fervor of those Eirik had received during the harvest wrestling tournament.

Asta kissed her husband's forehead then excused herself, pleading her condition.

"Brother, you have the better of me," conceded Eirik, gracious as he always was.

"Come, Faline." Gunnolf indicated the jug she carried. "Our horns require attention, and you have the means to satisfy us."

His bawdiness inspired snorts of laughter, but I took no pleasure in his lewdness. I worried that Asta may have heard her husband's remark as she made her retreat.

I knew Faline enjoyed attention and she seemed willing enough to claim Asta's place at the jarl's side, even if it were to play the whore rather than the wife. However, it was I Gunnolf looked at as he slapped her rump and drained his cup dry. My face must have shown my distaste, but he gave no rebuke, surveying me with lazy eyes.

With the drinking of more ale, a round of ribald jokes began and I felt inclined to take my own leave, but Eirik bid me stay and sit on his knee. This I did, though I soon regretted it. He'd drunk more than usual and became lustful before his men, bouncing me harshly upon his lap and reaching beneath my skirts.

He acted towards me almost as he had in the days of our first meeting, in the demeaning fashion of a master commanding his thrall. "Come, wench, you'll not deny me. You like me well enough in our bed."

"And in the fields, too," chimed one of the men, to the guffaws of his neighbors.

Eirik pulled aside the fine linen of my bodice, taking my breast in his hand, for all to see.

"Nay, Eirik." I endeavored to release myself, but he grasped me all the tighter as I struggled. Taking my nipple in his mouth, he laughed at my annoyance.

Seeing the leering grins of those about me, I slapped Eirik's cheek to make my escape. I pulled my clothes to cover myself. "I'm to bed and you may join me if you wish. If you prefer to sleep on a bench with your ale, then stay as you are."

Helka was never one to interfere in the jests of men, but she rose to my side, adding her voice in berating his lack of care.

Gunnolf howled with mirth. Slapping Eirik upon the back, he had a wicked gleam in his eye. "Best do as you're bid, little brother, since these women are your masters." He waggled his finger. "Perhaps you've lost your cock already and had better put on an apron."

At that, Eirik lurched to his feet and, within three steps, had grasped his axe. Helka reached to detain him, but he shrugged her away, eyes suddenly blazing.

"What say you?" Eirik roared. "I am man enough for any woman, and none the master of me."

Gunnolf rose to his feet. "None but I—the master of all Svolvaen."

The hall fell silent as the words were cast.

"Unless you go to chop wood, you'd best set aside your axe." Gunnolf's voice was filled with its own steel.

Eirik lowered his arm. I'd never seen him so—seeming not to know where to look nor what to say. He knelt upon the floor, bowing his head.

"Forgive me, my jarl. In my haste, I did not see the joke. The ale unbridled my temper, but my allegiance is yours, as ever."

Gunnolf reached down and took the axe from Eirik. "Beware, brother." He scanned the faces of his men, as if addressing not just Eirik but them all. "Do not allow that temper to be your undoing."

He ran his thumb across the sharp edge of the weapon.

"To do so will be to find the blade upon your own neck."

13

In the days that followed, Gunnolf made no further mention of his brother's rash outburst. Eirik resumed his usual graciousness before his jarl, but the merriment had been soured by the conflict between them. Perhaps some were afraid of incurring Gunnolf's wrath, of being humiliated as Eirik had been. Others, I believed, disliked seeing Eirik goaded.

My anger at Eirik's crude treatment of me soon abated, for I knew it had been the ale that had stirred his old ways. He took care not to repeat the indulgence and gave me naught to complain of. I didn't forget, however.

As *Jul* ended, Asta's appetite was poor, and she still seemed troubled.

"You must eat, my Lady," I would urge her, placing the most delicate morsels on her plate. She thanked me but consumed little.

Faline, meanwhile, seemed content. Often, she smiled as if she knew some pleasing secret, hugging it close-guarded to herself.

Svolvaen, too, had its secrets.

As the new year began, the blacksmith came to our door, stumbling in from the cold. "I must speak to the jarl."

Gunnolf beckoned him from his place by the fire. "Take some hot mead to warm you."

The blacksmith, Anders by name, accepted gladly and drank it down. "Two deaths." He wiped away the froth from his mouth. "My brother's youngest child and his wife's elderly mother. They've suffered an illness these past weeks and kept abed. They died in the night."

"I'm sorry to hear it." Gunnolf took a draught from his own horn. "And what malady was this?"

Ander shifted foot to foot. "I know not; only that it made some unsightly rash upon the skin."

My heart lurched.

"'Tis well that the weather has kept them indoors and away from others," said Gunnolf.

The blacksmith nodded his assent. "None other in the family seems affected but I'll keep my watch upon them."

He bowed to take his leave, but Gunnolf bid him stay. "The bodies?"

"We've buried them in the snow, for the great burning when the weather abates."

"Better not to wait." Gunnolf stroked his beard. "Take wood from the store for the pyre."

"I'll come." Eirik rose to don his cloak. "You and I may do it, Anders, with your oldest son's help. It will save your brother the burden. We'll stoke the fire high, to carry them onwards swiftly."

The snow whirled into the room as they departed, bringing with it a chilling gust. I knew what had killed the child and the grandmother. Left untreated, the poison had festered.

Gunnolf, Helka and Eirik were talking late around the fire, as they often did. Asta retired soon after the *nattmal*, though she'd barely touched her smoked herring nor the buttermilk.

I drew the brush through her hair until it shone.

"Lie down beside me, Elswyth," she bade. "I don't want to be alone."

Blowing out the lamp, I nestled to her back and slept, until I woke with cold in my bones. I'd lain upon the furs rather than under them and the night frost was hard.

Lowered voices muttered in the great hall, punctuated by the rising of one above the others.

Taking Asta's cloak, I crept to look through the shadows. Three backs hunched around the glow of the fire.

"With the first thaw, we must act." It was Gunnolf who spoke. "I wish revenge on Skálavík."

"What of Hallgerd's pact with their old jarl?" answered Eirik. "They've kept their word. Near thirty years have passed with peace between us."

"Time doesn't weaken a blood feud," snarled Gunnolf. "Our uncle Hallgerd lacked the stomach to bring battle to their door, but we must avenge our mother."

I'd never heard Gunnolf speak so violently and wondered what had brought this depth of feeling. Eirik had told me that his mother had died when he was barely three years old, but I didn't know the circumstances.

"We might join our blood with that of Skálavík." I heard Eirik say. "It would end the feud. Jarl Eldberg might accept Helka for his bride."

"Marry Eldberg!" she protested. "I'd rather lie with the hog."

"Nay," snapped Gunnolf. "Hallgerd is two years dead and I've waited long for this moment." He laughed but there was no mirth in it. "As to a marriage pact, the little birds I pay to tell me of our

75

enemies have sent notice that Jarl Eldberg has some new wife in his bed. An alliance is no longer possible."

Gunnolf took another swig of ale. "He'll pay for the actions of his father, as will all Skálavík."

The silence hung heavy before Eirik nodded. "Aye, brother. I understand your wish. However, I've no desire to lead us to empty defeat. Jarl Eldberg's warriors are strong."

"Asta's clan have pledged their help," added Helka.

"They have," conceded Eirik, "But the match was made by our uncle with an eye to her dowry. I don't trust her menfolk to fight to Valhalla's gates. They prosper only because they live upon an island easily defended."

"I'm ahead of you, brother. Before the snows came, I sent a petition to Jarl Ósvífur of Bjorgyn, offering Helka's hand to his son. You'll travel as soon as the way is clear."

Helka's voice was edged sharp. "And I have no say in the matter."

Gunnolf growled in displeasure; I wondered, not for the first time, at Helka's boldness.

She would comply with nothing against her will, but Eirik attempted to sway her, nonetheless. "Set aside your grief for Vigrid. Your unwed state is an insult to Freya and all the gods, who made women for the pleasure they bring to men and for the bearing of children."

I flinched to hear him say so for, if the bearing of children were a woman's duty, had I not also failed?

I couldn't see her face, but I imagined Helka's eyes blazing. "I'll never marry again, unless to a man of my own choosing."

"Enough!" Gunnolf's voice rose in a curse. "You'll have the man I put before you."

"The decision is wise, Helka," Eirik urged. "Leif Ósvífursson is renowned as a warrior and will become jarl in due course. It will be a good match."

Helka answered most coolly. "I might direct you to the same path, brother. I hear that young Freydís Ósvífursdóttir is in need of a husband. Why not an alliance forged from your marriage? She's newly reached her womanhood, I believe, and comely. You should take an honest wife. You've spent too many years casting your seed in random fields. If you won't marry for love, then do so for our people."

The betraying words turned my blood to ice, though I was in no position to rail at Helka. She'd never misled me as to my role in serving Eirik. Still, the thought of him laying this Freydís in the bed we shared made my bile rise.

I held my breath, waiting to hear how he'd answer.

He seemed about to speak but the words did not leave his lips.

Helka tossed her head in frustration. "I see that I must decide for us, brother. Your bravery only runs to violence, and not to matters of the heart." She jabbed at the fire. "I make no promise of compliance but, as soon as the weather allows, we'll travel to Bjorgyn. One way or another, we'll return with an alliance."

Gunnolf lifted the jug and filled each of their cups. "Here's to new allies, dear sister, dear brother. May you find them to your liking. If not, I suggest you do not return at all."

14

Helka donned her cloak and departed. Gunnolf too, rose. He took some steps towards the boxed room he shared with Asta before changing his mind. Turning away, he removed himself, instead, to the bench where Faline lay.

No doubt she'd heard all that had passed, as well as I. How gleeful she'd be. Not one word had Eirik offered to protest his love.

Helka had rightly warned me against believing Eirik ready to wed. However, I hadn't expected her to urge his marriage to another. I'd thought she would take my part—to wish my happiness as much as I wished hers.

I could foresee how it would go. Once in Bjorgyn, Helka would persuade Eirik to seal an alliance of marriage, so that she might be spared the contract herself. If Helka convinced him of her abhorrence of the match, Eirik's sense of duty would force his choice.

He didn't shift from the fire, continuing to stare into the embers. I watched him with neither the will to move nor speak. What could I say that would be worth the breath?

I'd struck a bargain and Eirik had kept his part. I wanted for nothing. He might have taken me against my will, making me his thrall. Instead, it had been my choice to accept whatever terms I found under his roof—not as his wife but as his consort. I'd made my choice willingly, to leave my homeland and travel to Svolvaen. I'd been eager to learn of my heritage from the father I'd never known; he who'd raped my mother and conceived my birth.

I'd embraced this path, wishing to learn about all that shaped my nature, but I was not ready to learn that the man I loved thought so little of me.

My position was precarious. It could do no good to dwell on my discontent, yet I couldn't set aside my heart's true yearning.

I walked to where Eirik sat. When he looked up, I saw an anguish I'd not expected, though I couldn't tell if he was pained merely for himself.

Leading him to our chamber, I undressed him and myself, until our bare skin touched. He guided my hand to where he wished it, but I was not ready to lose myself in lovemaking. Instead, I lay him down and curled my body to his.

"If you take a wife, what will become of me?"

"You'll stay with me." Eirik's voice was firm. "You're mine."

"You won't send me away? Marry me to another man?"

"Never."

I fought to contain my tears. "But how can it be? I cannot watch as another woman takes what I desire— marries, where I have no hope. And what of her, this Freydís? How can you expect to keep us under the same roof?"

"If I take her for my wife, she'll do as I ask."

"But you don't wish it, Eirik?" I'd never begged, but I could hold back no longer. "You want me to have your children? You want me to be with you, always?"

"Yes, my love, yes." His soft mouth found mine and his fingers stroked my hair. I felt the caress through all my body, wishing the reassurance of his physical love.

79

We sated our need, and there was unfathomable pleasure in his touch, breaking me apart until the world was tumbling and I was lost.

"You'll marry her." I whispered, afterwards.

"When the time comes for me to act, I'll know what I must do."

"And why must we obey your brother? Can we not leave? There are other lands, surely. A place we might go."

"You don't know what you're saying." His reply was resolute. "We must do what's best for Svolvaen—you and I both."

He placed his fingers on my lips, bidding me listen.

"When my mother told us to hide, Gunnolf carried me. We went to the forest, crouching among the trees. I didn't want to hear or see, but Gunnolf made me look, and Helka, too. We hid until there were no more flames. My uncle, Jarl Hallgerd, beat the Skálavík raiders into retreat, but my father fell, fighting."

Eirik's voice caught. "They took several of our women, my mother among them. Svolvaen emptied its stores and coffers for their release, and the pact was signed."

He said nothing for some moments, and I ached for him. I'd caused pain, making him remember.

"When she returned to us, she was changed. Grief for my father, I thought; perhaps something else I was too young to understand. A few months later, they found her in the fjord." His breath left him in a long sigh. "My uncle and aunt had no children, so we became theirs. As you know, on Hallgerd's death, Gunnolf received the jarl's mantle."

I kissed Eirik's fingers and moved them over my heart. "You serve him because it's what your uncle wished."

"And what my father would have thought right. It's my duty to serve Svolvaen and my jarl, even when I don't agree with his strategy."

"No matter that he wishes to lead Svolvaen into war against an enemy you may not be able to defeat?"

Eirik pulled me closer. "If it's my destiny to fight, I will."

"What if it's your destiny to die, Eirik?" Tears overtook me. There was so much I might say but I knew no argument would change how Eirik felt, nor the outcome. His bravery had won my heart, and the physical power of him. How could I change any part of what I loved?

His sense of duty was as real as the inked patterns upon his body—those markings that defined who he was. It was my history too; yet, half of me did not belong here, and I was not his wife. I was no better than his slave, albeit a willing one.

My voice trembled. "I can't lose you."

"Don't cry." He brushed my hair from my face. "I'll return, and we shall have many nights, my Elswyth."

He kissed me, murmuring his promises, but the words fell hollow, for what substance had they? I must take what was granted, having no power to demand more, but I feared an end to my happiness.

15

Weeks passed and the thaw came. The evening before their departure, we sat about the fire as we'd done many nights before. The flames leapt, and the shadows with them. We were subdued in our conversation, each consumed by our own thoughts.

Eirik fastened a leather thong about my neck, bearing an amulet. "The Gods shall watch over you, and Gunnolf."

I smiled weakly at that, for I'd no doubt that the jarl's eyes would be upon me.

I'd been angry with Helka for a long time. I could not put aside my belief that it would be Eirik who returned with a bride, rather than she with a groom. She was my friend, nonetheless, and I parted from her with a kiss.

The next morning, I watched them ride away. I wrapped my cloak about me to ward off the early morning chill, then went to rake the remnants of the fire. Nothing remained but blackened ash.

There had been other deaths over the frosted months, each accompanied by the same disfiguring blisters, but none spoke openly of the strange outbreak, which affected some and not others. The old and weak seemed to suffer most, and the very young. There was a rumor of dark magic, Astrid told me. Whispers of a curse upon Svolvaen bided behind closed doors.

The confinement of winter had curtailed the spread of the disease, but spring was on our heels. All hands were needed in the fields, and there could be no more hiding.

Having benefited several times from my healing draughts, Gunnolf bid me visit those who wished it. With the jarl's authority at my back, Svolvaen's doors opened to me, and I shared my remedies. I prevented sores from festering and eased the sting of open wounds, though a full cure evaded me. Some regarded me with suspicion and were reluctant to accept my touch; others were grateful for my care. I gave my time to all, and the blight ceased to be a private matter.

I refused to give up hope. The blooms were flowering afresh in the meadows, while plants' leaves unfurled in new growth. The answer, I felt sure, lay close to hand.

Despite this shadow hanging over Svolvaen, life continued. The fields needed ploughing, ready for their seed. Meanwhile, Gunnolf commanded that the fortifications of our settlement be strengthened, with a second row of outward-facing spikes added to our perimeter.

One day, around this time, I realized I no longer had the dried mushroom I'd picked so long ago—in my own forest, over the sea. It seemed an age ago that I'd been tempted to put its poison to evil use. That had been on the first night on which the Viking raiders had feasted in our hall, drinking my dead husband's ale.

It had been a foolish whim to bring it with me, and to keep it, secreted in a leather pouch in my pocket. I imagined it had dropped and fallen somewhere, without me having noticed. It was for the best.

Each day that passed took Eirik and Helka further away. I missed them both, but the needs of those about me were a distraction from the disappointment which ate my heart.

Both Gunnolf and Asta had need of my skill, for we were a house of troubled dreamers. My lady woke often with a mournful cry, though she shook her head when I asked her to unburden her fears. Whatever darkness filled her thoughts, she didn't wish to tell me of it. I treated her carefully, being wary of harming the growing babe.

My own nights were filled with the faces I saw through the day. In those sleeping hours, I roamed the forest, searching for the plant that would bring our cure. The wolf of old still prowled the shadows of my dreams, its gaze upon me, though it did not approach.

One night, Asta appeared in my forest reverie. She clutched the roundness of her stomach, her eyes beseeching, and I woke with beating heart. Hurrying to her chamber, I found her alone. Though pale, she was her own sweet self. I helped her in her toilette, then made her comfortable.

"You're near your time, my Lady." I unhooked the goatskin from the small window, placed where the roof met the low stone of the wall. She needed sunlight and the pleasant-scented air but was too weary to leave her bed.

"How attentive you are, my Elswyth." She smiled her thanks. "I know not where Faline gets to..." She let the thought trail away and I did not take it up.

"It's good to hear the birds and feel the warmth of the new season." Asta closed her eyes, resting her hands upon her belly.

"A fitting time for new life to enter the world." I spoke cheerfully, though I was worried that she carried not one babe but two within. If it were the case, the birth would not be easy.

"Time to redden the *hörgr* with sacrifices for Freya," Asta replied. "'Twas my own hand that did so at the last *Ostara*, dedicating them upon the forest's sacred stone."

"*Ostara?*" I hadn't heard of this festival.

"A time of dying to be reborn; of giving up old illusions and habits." She yawned, and I saw that she would soon be asleep again.

"I'll bring your *dagmal*," I said. "Remember that you must eat, my Lady."

I watched with interest as Svolvaen prepared for its festival. Unlike *Jul*, I sensed it would be a sombre affair. No one was willing to tell me what I wished to know, as if it could only be experienced and not explained.

I made my daily round, bringing more of my salve to Astrid. Torhilde had returned home at last—her husband finding he had need of her, after all. He'd become resigned to the marks upon her skin, having developed sores on his own body. Hers had responded well, as Ylva's had done, though they were not fully healed.

Astrid's youngest was growing well and was evidently of strong constitution. The babe had contracted not a single mark. The blight remained arbitrary in choosing its victims.

"Gunnolf has said that only those who are well are to attend the festival," Astrid told me.

"Do you mind?" I asked Ylva, but she blushed and turned away, leaving her mother to answer.

"I'm relieved, in truth," Astrid whispered. "*Ostara* is a night of mystery, when the gods bend close and whisper in our ear."

She led me outside. "The rituals take us back to the earth we came from, to the animal part of ourselves. It's not for children, or

85

for girls who've never lain before with a man. On *Ostara* night, there are no husbands and no wives; only men and women."

I guessed her meaning and was taken aback. Eirik had said nothing to me of *Ostara;* had given me no warning. I thought of the *Jul* festival and the many kisses he'd received. I'd refused to indulge my jealousy, but they held different significance now. I couldn't help but wonder if there were any women in Svolvaen who hadn't enjoyed the attentions of my warrior lover.

"It's up to you, of course," added Astrid. "The men won't touch you unless you invite them. But, beware when you do, for the lust of the gods is in them and you'll feel it in your own blood, too."

"And you, Astrid? Will you go?"

She gave a small smile. "I will. The ritual brings power to the soil and to our bodies. My bed is lonely. Who knows what *Ostara* will bring me..."

❦

Gunnolf cut a lock of Asta's hair, to burn on the sacred altar, since she was unable to attend. He drew the blade carefully through her silken tresses, placing the cut strands in his pouch.

"I shall remain with you, my Lady," I asserted. "You're too close to your time to be left alone."

However, the heaviness of Gunnolf's hand came to rest on my shoulder. "The ceremony invigorates us with gifts from Freya and all the gods. How can you heal others without that power?"

I kept my eyes upon the hem of Asta's gown.

"Faline shall stay and tend to your needs, wife." Gunnolf's thumb extended beneath my hair and found the bare skin at the back of my neck. "Under my eye, Elswyth will come to better understand our ways."

16

As the sun climbed, Gunnolf led us into the forest. The
horse's reins were loose in his hand, and I walked behind,
watching the swish of its tail.

It was a path Helka had never shown me. Light dappled
through the canopy, patches of warmth alternating with the shade
until the trees grew sparser. Entering an open glade, where the
spring sun penetrated, I felt the impatience of those about me.
Eyes glanced one to the next, alight with unspoken excitement.

My gaze was drawn to the *hörgr*: a huge altar stone flattened
along its upper edge.

The men lit a fire, stoked with debris from the forest floor and
ringed with stones. From branches cut and sharpened and driven
into the soil, we set make-shift frames, draping them with skins.
We'd brought food for feasting but none touched it.

"For afterwards." Astrid gave me a sly wink. "That's when you'll
be hungry." She unwrapped the laces of her boots, to leave her feet
bare. "Take off yours, and stay close," she directed, passing me a
wooden bowl.

"Kneel, women of Svolvaen." The jarl bid us approach the *hörgr*, while the men stood behind.

The smoky aroma was sweet, as if from the burning of rosemary and heather, but with a bitter undertone. It enticed me to breathe deep, drawing the seductive smoke inside my body. It left my head and body light. As the moments passed, the trees seemed to grow taller and the sunlight brighter.

"Give yourselves to Freya, on this day of *Ostara,*" the jarl continued. "Revel in her blessings, so that your bodies may ripen under her favor."

From his pouch, he took out the long strands of Asta's hair, throwing them into the flames, where they disappeared, as if they'd never been. "This symbol of womanhood I burn, asking Freya to accept our *blót.*"

At his nod, the men led the horse forward. "This animal I sacrifice, that Freya may bring prosperity to our crops, our livestock and our people."

The animal seemed to sense what was to come, for its eyes rolled suddenly in fear. It skittered away from the altar, obliging a tighter hold upon its rope. As Gunnolf raised a wide-headed axe, I shrank back, wishing not to witness the fatal blow.

"You must see," hissed Astrid, clutching my arm with surprising firmness. Her eyes were wide and bright. "Draw on our goddess Freya's strength."

I made myself look. Another of the men stepped forward, stunning the stallion just below its brow with a single stroke of his cudgel. Before the beast had time to fall, Gunnolf swung his blade to connect with its neck. The crimson spurt seemed almost to hang in the air, in that moment between life and death. Staggering, the horse let forth a rasping sigh and collapsed, the blood foaming to its mouth.

The slow arc of the jarl's second blow sliced through the thick air, meeting the neck once more. As the head was severed completely, I swayed, bumping against Astrid, who reached around my waist to support me.

"Life for life, we offer this blood to nourish the soil," declared the jarl.

"Do as I do." Astrid stepped forward, lowering her bowl to the tangled gore, catching the oozing scarlet. By the time I'd done the same, the pooled warmth upon the ground had stained my feet, sticky between my toes.

While we women assembled behind the altar, the men of Svolvaen ranged upon the other side. I'd never seen them so intent —as if in some trance.

"These women dedicate themselves to you, great Freya." Gunnolf raised his arms skyward. "As your willing handmaidens, fill them with the desire that drives all creatures of our world and, in their pleasure, make them fruitful."

He came to us in turn, dipping into the viscous liquid we carried, daubing each forehead. I trembled as he lowered his thumb into my own bowl of dark crimson.

It made me think of the day of falconry, when he'd marked me with the blood of the hare, and I dropped my eyes at the remembrance. I waited for his thumb to catch my lip, for his hand to raise my chin, that he might better see me.

When he moved on, I was left with the disturbing knowledge that I'd sought more of his touch.

The last of us was Bodil, and her eyes did not lower. Gunnolf drank from her bowl, leaving a smear upon his mouth. He placed his hands either side of her head and drew her into a kiss deep and long. I could almost taste the blood upon his lips, as if he were caressing my mouth, rather than hers.

He led her to the foot of the altar, where Bodil unclasped her apron, letting it drop. Having removed her tunic, she stood naked —pale and freckled, with her auburn hair loose over one shoulder. She was slender through the waist and hip, but her breasts were large, swollen from the milk with which she still fed her baby.

Gunnolf helped her step up, to lie upon the great stone. At his nod, the women moved closer, knowing their role, familiar with the ritual. The first raised her bowl, letting blood drip onto Bodil's stomach, then tipping further, running scarlet rivulets. The second bowl splashed her breasts, trickling to her throat, while the third cascaded down her abdomen, bloodying her pubis. Bodil gasped and arched her spine as if in raptures of desire.

She turned her head as I emptied my own bowl upon her stomach. Her eyes seemed to mock me—with her womanliness, with her proven fertility, with her seduction of the man I professed to call my own.

What did I have? An empty belly and an empty bed. Eirik had left. When he returned, it would be to bring home his new bride.

My reverie was interrupted by Gunnolf's voice, thick and slow and deep with lust. "Ripen our seed, Freya, in the soil of this woman's womb, and inside all our women." His face was transformed, eyes half-closed, while his palm stroked his erection.

Bodil cupped her breast while sliding her other hand through the slippery crimson, leaving a path down her torso. Her bloodied fingers reached inside her silken sheath, opening her lips.

Gunnolf gripped her raised knees, pulling her towards the edge of the stone to meet his penetration. It took but a dozen swift strokes before he groaned his release. Parting from her, his length bobbed wet, his lower torso marked with the blood from Bodil's body.

As the next man stepped into the jarl's place, Bodil extended her arms above her head. She took him willingly, lying still as he aligned his cock and thrust inside her. His strokes were more measured, deeper, bringing a quickening of her breath.

I could not look away, imagining the cold stone against my

own back. My mouth grew dry at the thought of taking Bodil's place, of surrendering myself to the same carnal abandon.

"Go, women," announced the jarl. "Find the men of your choosing."

Several immediately claimed their preferred partners, leading them off through the trees.

Astrid tugged my hand. "I know who I desire. Who will you choose, Elswyth?"

I looked again at Bodil, who was beckoning a third lover to approach. She took him in her mouth, while the other continued his slow strokes between her legs.

I fought the languor descending over my body. Stumbling to the edge of the glade, I heard Astrid call my name but, when I looked back, my eyes found not hers but those of the jarl.

His mouth curled in a lazy smile, revealing the bloodstains between his teeth.

17

Knowing only my need to escape, I ran from what I did not wish to recognize in myself. I emerged from the forest onto the open cliffs and gulped the crisp air, sobbing with relief at having left behind the strange enchantment that had threatened to overwhelm me. Burying my face to the cool soil, I slept.

He visited my dream, and we were wolves together, leaping through shadows. Far off, crows were cawing, and a night-wind rose through the trees. Bristling clouds swept the crescent moon, and something in me stirred, waiting to uncoil.

When I woke, he was beside me, his breath upon my neck, under the darkened sky. The scent of the strange smoke clung to him, and the faint aroma of coupling.

"No more running." He touched my collarbone above the yoke of my gown.

He was not the man I loved but it was not love I sought from him. I wished for the roughness of a kiss given in the service of jealousy, anger and lust; a kiss which would declare myself to be my own woman—slave to no-one. Despite my love, Eirik had abandoned me, just as he had so many women. He'd left me to fend for myself and so I would, without regard for him.

There was triumph in Gunnolf's eyes, for he was about to take what his brother presumed to own. He placed his hands about my throat, lifting my chin with his thumbs, drawing me upwards to meet his mouth. I was falling and there was no going back.

"Mine now," he growled.

His hands pushed away my bodice, baring the swell of my breasts to the cool air. Then, he was covering them with warm palms, thumbing my nipples. Breaking off our kiss, he dropped to take one hard point between his teeth. There, he devoured me, all the while pushing my skirts higher.

When he delved my wetness with a clutch of fingers, I whimpered. I wanted him inside, making me forget that I'd ever loved Eirik.

Above us, there was a blinding jolt of lightning, but I was too needy to pay it heed. The sky cursed us with its rolling thunder as I returned the roughness of his lust. As he gave me the column of his cock, I bit his lip and broke his skin with the drag of my nails. I pinched the underside of his buttocks to drive him harder.

He was wild and thorough, taking me so violently that I cried out in pain, but I had only one thought: that he must not stop.

He crushed my lips to his as he came, pulsing thick. His hands clasped my body to the depth of his final thrust.

Held beneath the weight of him, I clenched against each spasm.

18

The smoke from the sacrificial fire had affected my judgement. I'd had no warning of what *Ostara* would entail. If Eirik had given it any thought at all, what had he expected? Didn't he foresee that the jarl would take what he wanted, and I'd be powerless to deny him?

With such lies I tried to vindicate myself.

I'd proven faithless. Perhaps the village wives who'd looked at me askance had been right all along. I didn't deserve their respect, for I had little enough for myself. Wandering from room to room, I couldn't rest. I found duties outside and lingered in the barn. I willed Gunnolf to follow me, willed him to burn me again with his desire, to make me forget myself. Yet, when he had cause to pass me, I flinched away.

I could barely meet Asta's eye, though she treated me as she'd always done. Whatever she knew, or imagined, she did not betray it in her manner. Her heart seemed far lighter than my own, without the bitter burden of reproach, though her body grew ever weaker.

The baby, now grown large and eager to enter the world,

appeared to be taking her life-force to feed its own. When her pains began, I prepared the room, bringing water and linens, preparing the knife. I knew what was done, having more than once helped my grandmother deliver new life.

And yet, no baby came. Instead, Asta clutched her stomach and wretched bile, perspiration stark upon her brow.

"Can you hear it, Elswyth?" Her hand grasped my wrist with strength she couldn't spare. "It won't let me rest."

I soaked a flannel to cool her head and raised water to her lips. "There's no one here to hurt you," I soothed.

Still, she trembled and tossed, raking her skin so badly I had to bind her hands in cloth, tucking her nails inside her palms. Her eyes were unnaturally bright, following me about the room.

The black haw tincture I gave sent her, at last, into sleep, but she woke gasping for air. Now, she thrashed in her sweated bed, wracked in body and mind.

Gunnolf watched from afar, fearing to come near yet unwilling to leave her altogether. His face grew hollow, watching her slip away. He could not look at me, nor I at him.

My dreams were filled with Asta, walking always behind me, through the dark shadows of the forest. Her steps grew ever slower, hampered by her belly. Her eyes were filled not just with pain but with reproach, as if she knew that I'd wronged her.

On waking, I would hasten to her side—ready to beg forgiveness for my offence, willing to do whatever she commanded to make it right. Except, of course, there was no such remedy; no going back.

On the fourth day, Guðrún shook me at first light, for Sylvi wouldn't stir and her skin bore a speckled rash.

"Bathe her in cold water and ensure she drinks," I instructed.

As the village came awake, we saw that others had been visited by the same shadow, as if it had flown across the rooftops by night.

Had Svolvaen not endured enough? I'd seen this before, or

something much like it. The pox had touched our village one summer in my childhood. I remembered my grandmother brewing birch bark, yarrow, elderflower and meadowsweet to ease the fever. Borage too, which sprung between the brambles and nettles and fallen trunks. Its stems grew higher than my waist, its leaves rough and wrinkled.

Faline watched as I ladled the mixture into travelling pouches, bottles and jugs. She made no effort to help. Most of the time, she and I barely spoke, but the shared memory of our former home pressed hard on me. I knew her to be kin and regretted that we weren't closer.

"You remember how we came through the pox, years ago?" I prompted. "My grandmother treated us."

"I recall." Faline picked up one of the jugs, lowering her nose to the aroma of its contents. "Your aunt had taken my mother's place by then. She told me that, if I scratched, the scars would disfigure me, and I'd never find a husband."

She placed the remedy back upon the table. "I did everything they told me to but there never was a husband, was there…"

She and I, both, had been cheated, in various ways. I'd thought myself above her, at one time. I'd proven myself no better. I was worse, being a hypocrite. Faline, at least, made no pretense.

"Help me carry these?" I asked. "It'll be quicker together."

She regarded me a moment, then lifted a hand to her cheek. "I'm feeling a little weak… and hot. Perhaps, I should return abed…" She turned back after a few steps. "If you've any sense, you'll do the same. Let them look after their own."

I lay upon the floor, listening to Asta breathing through the night. While I heard her, I knew she lived.

She would swallow neither fish nor meat—only porridge and

honey. I coaxed this between her lips from my spoon and told her stories of my childhood: of the trees I'd climbed, and the joy of leaping into cool water in the heat of summer.

Waking before the dawn, she whispered. "Look after my baby." I lit the lamp and its flame quivered thin. Her cheeks bore twin flushes, though her face was paler than ever. "You and Eirik."

Had she forgotten the reason for his departure? Forgotten that there would be a marriage but that it would not be I who stood beside the groom?

"Beautiful in your wedding gown..." she mumbled, in her reverie of a future that could not be.

"And you'll be there to see it." I went along with the 'make-believe', promising her everything she wished. I brought her jewel box at her bidding.

"To wear on the day you become his bride." She fumbled among the trinkets until her fingers plucked two brooches, carved in bone and ringed in silver. One bore a bear and wolf, gripping one another in battle, surrounded by looping serpents; the other, a soaring bird, its wings and tail hanging low.

She placed them in my lap before resting back against her pillows. I sang to her while she closed her eyes.

The wick burned low, then lower, until the flame extinguished, and I was left in the dark. Somewhere beneath Asta's ribs, the unborn child pressed its fists to its blood-filled cage, but its fluttering jabs of arm and foot were in vain. Its battle was over before it had begun.

19

Only one other grieved as I did, though he never showed me his tears. I'd never doubted that Gunnolf loved her, though perhaps only in the way men do when they believe a woman to be too noble for them—resentment and adoration in equal measure. Had he once believed her goodness would elevate his own nature? It was how I'd felt, each day, in her presence. Instead, we'd both deceived her.

Asta had never treated me as a stranger. She'd been sister and mother both; more even than Helka, whose adventures took her beyond my sphere. And how had I repaid this kindness? I'd fallen so easily to temptation.

Now, she was lost to me in every sense. Taken to some realm beyond the living, she would surely know my sins. My self-loathing grew, for not only had I betrayed her, but I'd been unable to save her torment. It had dragged slowly, painfully, to the bitterest end.

Her symptoms had been strange. Not quite those of the pox, though she'd displayed many of the signs. Instead, her body had turned against itself without apparent cause.

I washed and dressed her for the final ceremony: for the burial she'd wished. One of her brooches I fastened to her robe of purest white. She'd given me so much, and I wished to place something I treasured in her resting place. The other I pinned to my shoulder. I hoped she'd find peace, embracing both her children in death—her son, and the unborn babe within her body.

Gunnolf carried her in his arms to the edge of the forest, to the hole he'd dug himself beside the resting ashes of their child; she weighed little, and he was strong.

It was a quiet affair, for so many in the village were affected by the pox, keeping to their houses in sickness or in tending others. Gunnolf said naught as he laid his wife's richest jewels upon her breast, and her lute beside her. He crouched down to whisper his farewell, for her ear alone. He then took up the spade, his face hard in sorrow, casting the soil upon her body. I shuddered to see it fall, feeling its weight as if it were I who lay in the cold ground, buried slowly by the earth.

The men would later build a mound above: a resting place fit for the jarl to join his lady and their babes, when the time came, Guðrún told me.

In the days to come, I attended the sick, mixing salves and tinctures. There was too much death. Illness took several of the younger babes, too feeble even to cry their hunger.

Gunnolf did not come near, except to command stronger draughts for sleep. There was danger in increasing the potency of the valerian root. It would do more harm than good, I warned. Headaches and dizziness would plague him, however strong his heart. His mind, in anguish, would rebel, losing its former reason.

He cast my cautions aside, shadows beneath his eyes telling me of his need. I gave what he asked, understanding that longing to find oblivion, each waking bringing the misery of remembrance. I, too, wished to escape, to no longer know myself. My strangled remorse was more than I could bear.

I dreamt of rotting leaves and the drip of water through earth and rock, soil cold in my mouth and crawling things. I looked into the dark, and it slithered inside.

20

I knew that they talked about me, despite all I'd done for them. It wasn't enough that I'd treated their sores and tended them through the pox. I heard the whispers as I passed their homes. I saw the narrowing of their eyes and heads turned from me.

Lady Asta had been under my care, and she'd died. I was to blame.

Visiting Astrid, it seemed our friendship had grown cooler. Neither of us spoke of *Ostara* night. I knew not what to say.

Leaving her, I noticed Bodil sitting outside her own door. With a length of cloth in her lap, her fingers plucked with her needle. She raised her chin and met my eye, her lips drawn thin, unsmiling.

I wished suddenly to be far away, to be just myself, unanswerable to anyone. My feet took me through the fields of new shooting barley, rippling in the late afternoon breeze. The trees were already trailing long shadows, the swallows dipping and looping against a sky streaked through with violet cloud.

However far I walked, there was no escape from my thoughts— from all that had happened and what might be to come. I fingered the amulet at my throat. Eirik had vowed to return, had worshipped my body as he made his promises of protection and love. Did those promises have any worth?

With Asta gone and Eirik soon to return with his bride, what place was there for me? Was I destined to perform the most menial tasks, like Sylvi and Guðrún, without hope of a home of my own, a husband, children? And then I remembered how I'd lain with Gunnolf, willingly, knowingly, and I was filled with shame. What sort of woman was I? If I suffered now, it was no more than my due.

With dusk falling, I returned up the hill. Sylvi was still suffering from the pox. Gunnolf had sent her to Helka's empty home during her recovery. It left Guðrún with more work than she could manage. It was selfish of me to have stayed out so long. Faline, I knew, would help with only the easiest of duties.

I returned past idle-grazing livestock, skirting behind the huts. Before I rounded the corner, I heard them, sitting just beyond, not far from the longhouse. There was still much for me to learn of Svolvaen's language, but I understood the men well enough.

"... a whole houseful of women to comfort him now..."

"No wonder he looks like he doesn't sleep."

They chuckled at that.

"I'll take the dark one off his hands when he's bored with her..."

"The blonde for me," said another. "If she's good enough for Eirik, she'll be good enough to suck my old cock."

My face grew hot, but I couldn't claim to be surprised. I knew men well enough—how they talked of women.

"He tired of her quickly, didn't he? Won't be long now before he's back, and with some other pretty wench to warm his bed."

"About time... though she'll have to be more than pretty to keep his sword from finding other sheaths."

As they laughed again, the bile rose in my throat. I'd only heard what I already knew—that I was but one of many lovers to have entertained Eirik for a short while, before his attention was drawn elsewhere. No doubt, he'd told Bodil he loved her, too... and all the others.

It was impossible to escape the truth. No matter my anger and my faithless deceit, I loved Eirik.

I lay awake that night and thought of the man who'd pleasured me in so many ways, pouring his desire into me. The bed was cold without him, despite the generously piled furs.

Whose body was warming his as I lay alone? There would be some companion—some thrall to pleasure him, or more than one. Perhaps he was already wed, and his new bride spooned beside him, tasting what I'd so lately enjoyed. Such thoughts were fruitless, but they returned time and again.

The evening had not been a pleasant one. It seemed so long ago that we'd spent time in storytelling and song, the men bantering and the women teasing. Hardly possible that these walls had gathered Svolvaen's people so recently in festivity, at Yuletide.

Gunnolf's mood became ever sharper, finding fault with each dish served to him. Even his favored men from the village—summoned to keep him company, to play dice and share their news—were unable to lift his spirits. He sent them away, his words harsh where there was no need.

Faline dropped a dish of bread, for which Gunnolf gave her a clout, sending her to the floor. He raised her by the hair, saying she was a useless wanton—that he would cast her out and forbid any household to take her in, that he would tie her to a tree in the forest and let the boar and wolves find her.

Her eyes had flashed in resentment, but she'd kept her silence. She'd pinned her fortune to Gunnolf just as surely as I had to Eirik, and what awaited us now? She'd shed no tears at our Lady's passing; perhaps, she'd thought Asta's death would be her making. For all her wiles, Faline was no wiser than I, both now slaves to the whim of the jarl.

I dozed, at last, but was stirred by a creak and a sigh, a moan, long and low. From outside, I thought—some animal in pain, one of our livestock. The wall behind me adjoined the stable and there were two calves due to be delivered. The young lad who slept with them would call for help if it were needed. I strained my ear but there was no voice on the wind.

And yet, something was amiss.

Slipping on my cloak, I entered the main hall. The ceiling stretched above, a reaching chasm of darkness in which some bird or bat was trapped, flapping through the rafters. The embers glowed in the firepit.

I paused to listen, looking into the recesses of the room. To my left, Guðrún was snoring. All else was quiet but I sensed something. I could not discern what or who it might be, but it was outside, I was sure.

I eased the door open, careful to avoid it creaking. The moon's illumination seemed unnaturally bright after the darkness of the longhouse, enough to show me the slope of the hill and the outlines of houses further down.

There was a screech from some night bird—an owl most likely —which drew my eyes to the edge of the forest. In the moonlight, it appeared closer, as if the trees had shuffled forward as we slept.

But there was no creature, huddled and wounded, lingering beyond; nor some scavenger, sniffing for scraps. No sound from the stable.

There was nothing but the breeze of the night hours, shivering the far-off trees. Nothing but my own breath, and the beating of my heart.

21

F aline filled the jarl's cup once more then withdrew to the corner of the room. Her cheek bore a bruise, her eye darkened above, the brow cut. I'd given it three stitches to close the gash, for which she'd grudgingly given her thanks.

Gunnolf had been drinking since that morning. He was as likely to become violent as melancholy. I watched from the alcove of the pantry, Sylvi and Guðrún beside me.

A few of the other men had joined him in a game of chance.

He cupped the dice close, whispering to them before casting, but the outcome was the same as it had been on every throw. "To Hel's realm with this! There's Loki's trickery here, or one of you has replaced the dice."

"Peace," soothed one of the others. "'Tis but a friendly game. We may play some other if you prefer."

"Damn this foolishness and take up your weapons," Gunnolf staggered some steps to grasp his double-handed axe from where it hung. "It's been too long since we practiced our skills. What manner of men are we if we forget how to fight?"

"My Jarl, now is not the time," urged another of the men. He rose warily, his gaze upon the blade in Gunnolf's hand. "We're in our cups and may not judge as we should. We wouldn't wish an injury on our brethren."

"A man should be always ready." Gunnolf planted his feet. "I'm not my uncle. I'm not weak, like Hallgerd."

"You're the bravest and strongest of men," agreed the first. "With pleasure, we'll polish our swords on the morrow and join you outside."

Gunnolf swung the axe in a great arc that threatened to meet with their heads. Stumbling under its weight, he brought the edge down, embedding it with a mighty thud in the age-stained table.

All had risen, moving beyond the jarl's reach. They looked wildly one to the other, as aghast as we women.

"I see into your hearts." Gunnolf tugged fiercely on the weapon, cursing as he tried to release it. "You've no stomach for battle. You're as slippery as eels, making excuses for your fear!"

Though he clearly spoke in drunkenness, the declaration was the greatest of insults. A man's honor was everything, and not to be challenged lightly.

There was a grumbling of displeasure, but none raised his voice above the others. Their eyes were still upon the axe, which Gunnolf had now freed and was passing from one hand to the other.

"When I call on you to attack Skálavík, which of you will take your sword and bathe it in enemy blood?" Gunnolf lurched forward. "When I put Eldberg's head on a spike, what will you be doing?"

The men scattered. Some bounded for the door; others dodged the jarl's swinging axe, leaping away to escape his rash attack.

"Run away, weasels," he shouted after them. "Get out of my sight. You're not fit to call yourselves men, let alone warriors of Svolvaen!"

As the last scurried to safety, Gunnolf crashed the door closed with his shoulder and flung his axe across the floor. Finding his cup, he drained it dry.

"More ale!" he shouted.

Faline, hidden far in the corner of the room, shrank from him. I couldn't blame her, for I wished to do the same. He was in no state for company. Yet, some compulsion bid me do as he'd requested.

"Are you the only one brave enough to face me?" Gunnolf's eyes were steely.

I refused to bow my head or look away, and he returned my unflinching stare. Tension lay heavy in the space between us. At last, he held out his cup, indicating for me to fill it. I willed my hand to remain steady, vowing not to give him the satisfaction of seeing my fear.

His draught was deep, and the ale ran down his beard. Wiping his mouth with his sleeve, he grimaced, tossing the empty cup to the floor.

"What is a man to do, when all about him are cowards?"

"You're tired, my Jarl. Take the rest you need."

"Rest!" He flung back his head and gave a hollow laugh. "Sleep brings no rest." A shadow crossed his face. "Better to stay awake and find diversion."

Shrugging off his jerkin, he flopped back onto one of the deep benches. He propped his head upon his arm, keeping his eyes directed at me.

"Do you wish diversion, Elswyth? Or do you prefer to sob to your pillow, pining for the man who has left you?" Gunnolf's smile was crooked. "Be assured, he shall be too occupied elsewhere to give you a moment's thought."

He waited for my answer, but I gave none. He'd hit his target, voicing what I was only too ready to believe. Bitterness rose in me, towards Eirik and Gunnolf, though I was most angry with myself. I'd been a fool to believe that Eirik could love me in the way I wished him to.

Gunnolf stroked his beard as he spoke, and a new wickedness entered his eyes. "My brother and I always shared everything. Shall we not share you?"

"I've already tasted that wine, my Jarl, and found it lacking sweetness." I lowered my eyes for, despite all, I felt the tug of my womb for him. The lust which had consumed me at *Ostara* had brought me shame and self-loathing. Yet, I hadn't forgotten the satisfaction of that terrible abandonment, however fleeting.

"Sweetness isn't what I'm offering." Gunnolf's mouth twitched in a disdainful leer.

Under his scrutiny, the clothes peeled back from my body, the skin from my bones, showing all I wished to hide.

"What is it you want?" My voice trembled.

"I'll show you." He clicked his fingers, summoning not I but Faline.

She came forward, knowing, I supposed, that to refuse would bring worse consequences.

"An obedient creature, when she wants to be." Gunnolf cupped beneath her chin, surveying the injuries of his making. The next moment, he spun her about. Pushing her to bend over, he raised her skirts.

He must have beaten her quite recently, for the welts were still livid across her buttocks—blue, without any hint of yellowing. He unclasped his belt and pulled the leather through.

My mouth grew dry, waiting for him to raise it to her poor skin. There was no love lost between Faline and I, but I'd no wish to see her suffer.

"It's shameful for a man to harm a woman, or for him to take her body when she has no desire."

"You think this one has no desire?" Gunnolf slapped Faline's backside and I winced to see her flinch. "She likes to fight but she likes fucking even more… and she is made for fucking."

He lingered over the last word and pulled the belt tight

between his hands. However, instead of raising his arm to strike her with its edge, he pulled her hands awkwardly behind her back, wrapping the belt's length around her wrists.

He lowered his mouth to the bruise on the rounded cheek of her behind and bit the flesh savagely, evoking her sharp intake of breath. He next kicked her legs wider, before entering her roughly with his fingers. Faline did not struggle; rather, she lifted her rump to encourage his entry.

Gunnolf then let his trousers drop and took his erection in hand. I expected him to jab inside, to take her brutally. Instead, he ran the slick head through Faline's slit. He teased her with half-thrusts, rubbing against her tender nub.

"Please..." I heard her whimper.

The last time I'd seen Faline taken, it had been Eirik burying himself inside her—upon the banqueting table of my husband's hall, cheered on by every Northman present. Faline had taken many that night, but her prize had been Eirik: he the one she'd most desired.

Gunnolf aligned himself, claiming with one smooth motion, pushing deep before easing back to enter again. Faline moaned in response, whispering again, as if to herself. "Please..."

A heat began to burn me—partly of anger but also arousal.

"There's more than one place to fuck a woman, of course." Gunnolf's voice was cold as he withdrew, slick with her juices. He pressed against her anus, holding Faline firm about the hips. She squirmed briefly before he pushed past her initial resistance.

Something kept me there, watching as his buttocks clenched and relaxed. Faline uttered low groans, as of a creature caught in a trap yet with no desire to escape. He kept his rhythm until the end, culminating in his final convulsions of pleasure.

I hadn't moved from where I stood. I'd waited, with the growing knowledge that when he turned to me, I would submit.

I'd pour out all my bitterness—at Eirik, as well as his brother.

Gunnolf was just a man; I'd use him to sate my need. Gunnolf wished a slave to command but I would command him: take him, own him!

I desired a man inside me again, but also hungered to lose myself in the act. We'd consume each other, in wrath and fury, rather than love.

Gunnolf withdrew from Faline's body, presenting a cock no longer fully rigid yet still emboldened.

"You're an animal." Picking up the nearby jug of ale, I cast the contents to drench his groin. I knew it would fire his passion.

In a single step he was upon me, his hands wrenching my shoulders. Growling his ire, he laughed low. "Exactly as you wish."

He yanked the front of my dress, breaking the clasps. He then dragged down the shift beneath, tearing the clothes from me as I stood. I did nothing to defy him, my own hands helping until I was naked.

I revelled in his palms moving over my breasts, cupping my buttocks, squeezing my flesh. I cared not that Faline watched as I gave myself to him, nor that her eyes burned with displeasure.

I clasped the great muscles of his arms, steadying myself against the roughness of his mouth. I was opening my legs even before he lay me upon the bench. His piercing brought a moan of pleasure I couldn't conceal. I wanted his violence. My skin was hungry for his raking teeth.

He crushed me to his chest as he ejaculated, with a cry to match my own, as we both tumbled into the abyss.

22

I knew Gunnolf's soul ached. There was no remedy. His anger was another version of my own. We sated mutual grief and savage passion. Each bruise he gave me was a brand for my many sins. They marked the slow death of my heart.

His moods were volatile and violent. He lashed out before burying his head upon my lap. He told me of the first days of his wedded life, and before. His uncle had arranged the marriage. A contract of alliance, of course, and for a rich dowry. Nevertheless, Gunnolf had been won over by Asta's loveliness, her composure, her grace. She'd been his prize.

Now, he lamented all he should have said and done. "Did she die, Elswyth, because I failed to show my love? Is it this she cannot forgive? Her beauty is buried and rotting, yet she does not rest; nor will she allow me peace."

I mixed the sleeping draughts he demanded. Even so, he tossed in haunted dreams.

I saw her too: fingers bone-white, eyes hollow and searching.

Each moment of sleep took me to the forest, where the trees

lead me in circles. She was always there; now close at my shoulder, then behind. It was no longer her belly that she clutched but a bundle in her arms, which she thrust towards me. Within was the grey face of her swaddled baby, without breath or life. Her expression held pain and reproach.

I couldn't shake the fear that I'd not been asleep but had been looking through the darkness at her face.

The rising sun brought the promise of Summer. Its warmth should have lifted my heart, as it did those of the children who ran outside, eager to make up for lost days.

I'd helped Svolvaen recover from the pox—easing debilitating fever and the rash, but I could scarce rejoice. Asta's death, and my betrayal of her, remained a torment to me. As for my healing skills, I began to doubt them. I'd found no cure for the disfiguring sores; my treatments remained no more than a temporary salve.

Meanwhile, my friendship with Astrid had floundered. We'd hardly spoken since *Ostara* night. Astrid had confided in me during her anguish; I'd pulled away in mine.

Answering her door, Astrid kept me on the threshold for a moment before inclining her head to invite me in. She shifted the wriggling baby from one hip to the other. "Take a seat. You know you're welcome."

I deserved the sharpness in her tone. I'd neglected her, and Ylva.

"Fresh pulled an hour ago." Having lowered the little one to the floor, she poured some milk and handed me a cup. "Ylva's taking the goats down to the meadow, so it's just us."

I sipped the creamy liquid, still warm, and smiled my thanks.

"You've been occupied, I hear." Astrid took the stool across from me. She clucked her tongue. "It's no more than anyone would expect, I suppose—with you sharing the same roof, and Eirik gone these many weeks."

All Svolvaen probably knew; there was little that could be hid. When I didn't reply, Astrid rose to stir the contents of her pot, suspended over the fire.

"I didn't intend..." I couldn't bring myself to explain. Whatever was happening between myself and Gunnolf, I didn't know how to describe it.

"The other—that Faline—not enough for him; he's got to have you, too?" Astrid looked pointedly at the discoloration on my neck. "And both of you feeling the heel of his hand. He needs another wife, of course. Although that won't stop a man like him."

I'd loosened my hair about my shoulders, but the marks were difficult to hide. There were more on my wrists.

Astrid lowered her voice. "The jarl has told the men to farm only in the morning. They're to fell timber the rest of the day, to extend fortifications by the harbor; on pain of flogging if they don't."

I frowned to hear it.

Astrid lowered her voice. "They're looking for Eirik's return. It's him the men love; he who should be jarl."

It was no surprise, but I shifted uncomfortably. Such talk brought trouble. Besides which, I'd tried hard to push away thoughts of Eirik, to convince myself that I'd stopped waiting for him.

"There's something else; something not right." Astrid hesitated, then looked away. Taking up the poker, she stoked the flames beneath her cooking pot.

"What is it, Astrid?"

"I'm not sure I believe it. I shouldn't have said..." She bustled to the pantry, returning with an armful of vegetables. As she chopped, the knife trembled in her hand.

"It's not more illness?"

"No. Nothing of that sort." She kept her eyes downcast, slicing into the pale flesh of a turnip. "Not any illness that can be cured..."

"What are you saying?"

"There are whispers, but I've not seen it myself... It was wrong of me to say."

I came to stand beside her. "I must know, Astrid! It's something affecting Gunnolf? Affecting me?"

"Perhaps, yes..."

My heart lurched.

"She was never strong but, still... we didn't expect it. We were waiting for the baby to be born. Even though she lost the first, we thought it would be alright this time. Asta wasn't one of us, but everyone respected her—loved her, even."

Astrid's eyes darted to mine, her words tumbling, urgent. "You did, too, didn't you, Elswyth? You would never have hurt her..."

"No." My voice scratched in my throat. "I would never have hurt her."

Astrid shook her head. "Then it can't be you. She's come back, but it's not for you."

The room grew smaller in that instant, the walls moving closer. "Come back?"

Astrid let drop the knife. "When there's something not right—a hurt the person can't forgive, a betrayal, some wrongdoing...when they can't let go..."

I grasped the edge of the table. I didn't trust myself to speak.

"That's what they say. It must be something terrible, don't you think, to bring her back? A spirit isn't restless without reason."

I summoned all my strength. I had to know everything. "Someone has seen... her, Asta, in Svolvaen?"

"At the top of the hill, near the edge of the forest and..."

"You must tell me, Astrid!"

She flinched at my raised voice. "Around the jarl's longhouse."

The room swayed around me. No matter what I told myself, I could not escape. My knees buckled and I fell to the floor, dissolving within the dark tide.

23

R aised voices roused me. I couldn't make out the words; wasn't sure that I wanted to. I wasn't asleep, nor awake; somewhere between. I was comfortable. If only they would stop shouting. I wanted to remain curled as I was, hidden, shutting out the others.

I remembered what Astrid had told me. The sins of the past were not forgotten, and Asta did not lie peacefully in her grave.

Who but I was to blame? I'd loved her... but had some dark corner of my being wished her to die? Hadn't I coveted her status, and the way in which she was universally loved?

As for the jarl, I was no naïve maiden, my virginity seduced away. I'd known what I was doing. I'd become his willing lover, overtaken by a madness of self-loathing, fed by emotions I could barely fathom. He and I were alike in ways I didn't want to recognize. We were both capable of fury. Whatever excuses I conjured, I couldn't escape my guilt.

Someone was sobbing, someone shouting; words coming closer.

"...dark forces, in the forest. Just like her grandmother." It was a voice filled with hate. "...goes out at night, looking for her crea-tures, picking plants for her spells."

There was a murmur through the room.

"...bewitched Eirik... made him bring her here... put magic on my father before that... been casting her enchantment on you, Gunnolf... she wants Asta's place... was chieftain's wife once and wants to be again."

"Wake her." The speaker was gruff, his voice commanding.

Hands raised me up, splashed water in my face. I shied from returning but those hands were insistent.

Someone pinched the inside of my elbow. "Wake up, witch!"

Faline raised something to my face. Her serpent eyes lit. "I found what you've been carrying in your pocket! A deadly mush-room, and one piece missing!" Her mouth was voluptuous even as she spoke venom.

I shook my head in confusion. I hadn't anything in my pocket. The mushroom had been lost weeks ago, before *Ostara* night. I couldn't remember when I'd last seen it.

"What say you?" It was Gunnolf's voice, full of pain. "Was it your scheme all along? To kill whoever stood in your way? To seduce whichever man could most advantage you? What mischief did you plan?"

The mushroom in Faline's palm looked much like the one I'd picked, long ago, when I'd walked in the forest with Helka. The red rim beneath the cap was distinctive.

I'd brought it with me, across the sea—a symbol of unused vengeance. I could have killed a host of warriors with this tiny mushroom. Had some part crumbled into Asta's food? Had I poisoned her? I thought back to her symptoms: stomach cramps, nausea, vomiting bile, and the itch across her skin. Not the pox at all, but the gradual, agonizing failure of her body.

The horror of it tore at my chest so I could hardly breathe. It wrenched my gut like the devil's own claws. The mushroom was mine.

"The guilt is in her face!" Faline spat the words. "Look! I dare her to deny it!"

"It's true," declared Gunnolf. "I see it, now. Only a conscience wracked with shame could look thus."

"No..." My tongue was thick in my mouth. What could I protest against? Had I not wanted position and power? Had I not envied? Kept secrets? And who but I had tended Asta?

"Murderess!" Faline hissed, as they led me away.

24

Many gathered, watching as the jarl's men led me to the harbor, with my hands bound. Wrongdoers were beaten, but what of murderers? What of witches?

They secured me to the whipping post. Not in the position for flogging; I faced forward, my back pressed to the old wood.

I was used to seeing Gunnolf in many moods; now, I saw the cold resignation of his heart. He desired another to take the blame, to ease his sense of guilt.

My mouth was dry with fear, but I tried to avert my gaze from the many who looked upon me, to focus only on the jarl. "I loved our Lady Asta. I did all in my power to care for her and the baby."

I endeavored to hold Gunnolf with my eyes, to convince him of my sincerity, but he turned away.

Scouring the crowd, I searched for some sign of support. Had I not tended their children, treated them in their sickness? For that, hadn't I earned their trust? I hardly recognized them now: women and men ready to turn against me. I could hear their mutterings: '… not our kind… thinks herself too clever'.

The sun had already dipped low but sweat trickled down my

back. My mouth tasted sour. "If I could bring her back, I would..." My pleading voice sounded thin.

I thought I'd escaped those who didn't understand me, to have found a new life, among new people. I'd deceived myself, for I remained as much a stranger as ever, mistrusted and suspected of ill-doing.

Torhilde was pushing through, calling my name. Astrid followed with Ylva, carrying the little one. Astrid whirled to challenge the crowd. "Elswyth would never hurt anyone! Have you forgotten what she did for us?"

Torhilde's voice shook as she spoke. "Elswyth showed me compassion when my own neighbors had none. Only Astrid took me in; only Elswyth would dare look upon my affliction. Didn't she risk her own health, entering your homes?"

Drawing back the yoke of her gown, Torhilde revealed the dull redness of a still tender sore, part-healing. "How many of you have these on your body? Hasn't Elswyth tended you?"

A sob rose in my throat. How brave she was, and in loyalty to me. Whatever was to happen, it gladdened me to know that I wasn't alone.

The young woman who next stepped forward wore her hair loose—a cascade of auburn-red. "Your sores are not yet recovered, Torhilde. You still rely on this woman, hoping she'll heal them." The look Bodil gave me was arrogant, her eyes filled with enmity. "Perhaps she has you where she wants—reliant upon her to heal you. She feeds upon your gratitude."

She spoke with relish, as if she'd waited long to smear my name with the basest of accusations. "How many others are the same— hiding what shames them, dependent on this interloper, waiting for her cure? She has no noble blood or claim to higher status, yet she has you all as her thralls."

"She's a witch!" sneered Faline. "She probably caused your sores. Don't let her fool you. She cares only for herself."

Another took up the cry. "Caused the sores and the pox, too!"

I looked again to Gunnolf. Would he credit such slanders, based on nothing but Faline's word and the vindictiveness of Eirik's former lover? There was no softening to his expression but nor was there malignance. His thoughts were impenetrable.

"I trust neither of these foreign women," said Bodil, "But this dark-haired one knows the other well. If she warns us of this woman's ill-intent, I believe her."

Faline cast me a triumphant glance, barely able to conceal her glee. Running forward, she thrust her face close to my ear. "No Eirik to save you now, but don't worry; I'll keep him warm for you, when he returns... I've passion enough for both brothers."

It was suddenly clear to me. Another had sat with Asta, on *Ostara* night. Soon after that, she suffered the cramps that convulsed her body. The mushroom had been lost not long before. Faline had found it, surely— had recognized its nature, or guessed why I'd kept it. I'd been blind.

"Enough!" Gunnolf raised his hand. "What we cannot know, the gods shall decide. Tie her to the stacks at the end of the pier. If she survives high tide, it will be they that save her."

"No!" I struggled against the arms that carried me through the parting crowd. I caught sight of Astrid's stricken face, her cheeks wet with tears.

I shouted my innocence, but the crowd's growing clamor drowned my words.

The stacks would be covered within a few hours. I'd be left in the dark, gasping for breath as the chill water lapped over my mouth, then my nose. There would be none to save me and I'd have no power to save myself.

25

The sun left the sky and the slim moon rose. My hope sank as I waited beneath the small stars sliding cold through the dark. The water made insidious progress, to my chest, my shoulders.

At first, I'd wondered if someone might be brave enough to follow their conscience. They might steal unseen through the village, to untie the cruel rope which wrapped about my waist and hooked over the outer stack of the pier.

A few had lingered, to watch me lowered into the fjord's chill embrace, to call names from the safety of the shore. None wished to come too close. After all, I was a witch, was I not?

Even Gunnolf had kept his distance. Whatever we'd shared, it had not been built upon love.

Eirik's amulet nestled in the hollow of my throat. If I saw him again, in the next life, I'd swear my love and my regret. Anger and resentment had brought bitter pleasure. I'd been fated neither for happy marriage nor the security of devotion.

I was solitary, in the shadow of the grey night.

The tide was almost fully in. The waters stretched from this place to the land of my birth. I prayed to my old God and then to Freya, Frigg and Fjorgyn: the female gods. If they had no ear for my suffering, then none would.

Would they punish Faline as I was being punished? We each had our sins. She'd acted from jealousy—from desiring what lay out of reach. Her grudge had long simmered, stored away until her spite could be indulged. Even in her wickedness I pitied her, for she'd find no contentment.

The clouds drifted over the moon, obscuring what little light was to be had. It was quiet, as if Svolvaen had melted far away. I was alone with the lap and splash of waves against the fishing boats, gently rocking in their moorings on either side of the pier. I thought back to what Astrid had told me—that Asta's restless spirit walked. No one wished to be outside, even to watch the final breaths of a witch, as the water claimed her life.

If Asta wished revenge, it was done, for my life could now be measured in gasping breaths. I tipped my chin and closed my eyes as the black waves stroked my lips, theirs the last caress upon my skin.

And then, something swept my leg—the smooth glide of a fish, or a feathering of seaweed. It skimmed silken against my arm, brushing lightly upon my wrists. My body slipped beneath the water as the bonds loosened, and I tasted the briny sea. Kicking my legs brought me to the surface, gasping for air, with my heart pounding.

I knew not who, or what, had intervened. Some creature sent by the gods or their own divine hands. I could not think—only rejoice at the chance given to me.

My skirts were heavy as I swam, my shoulders stiff and my chilled body leaden, but force of will drove me towards the shore. The push of the waves helped bring me to the shallows until my knees scraped shingle. I dragged myself beyond the movement of the water, glad to feel the pebbles beneath me and the brisk nip of the night air.

There was barely a sigh of wind, the world quiet but for the breaking waves and a far owl calling. I was exhausted to my bones, yet the beat of my heart was loud. I was exhilarated, for I was alive.

I could not remain thus for long. One thing was certain; that I must take action. I might present myself to Gunnolf and all Svolvaen as having escaped the tide's reach. The gods had saved me, proving my innocence. Yet, I feared the malevolence of Faline and Bodil. They wouldn't rest until their spite was sated, and they'd have no trouble finding ears. The seeds of doubt had been sown, even among those who'd shared my friendship.

I needed time to plan and a place of safety from which to do so. My first thought was of Astrid; she, I could trust. Alongside Torhilde, she'd spoken for me when so many were ready to believe ill. She'd hide me if I asked, but this I would not do. How could I place her in such a position?

High on the shingle was Helka's little boat—the one in which she'd taken me sailing through the fjord. How long ago that day seemed, when I'd thrilled to speed with the wind and shared her delight in the success of our fishing. I remembered her showing me the cave—her own special place, where the ledge ran flat and deep.

Might I manage the vessel alone, with the oars rather than the sail? The moon's slender crescent was in my favor, breaking only momentarily through the cloud. None was likely to see me, even were they to look out.

The pebbles shifted as I hauled the boat by the bow. Every part of my body ached but I made jerking progress to the water's edge. Finally, I was wading out, light-headed with relief.

My sodden skirts slapped the deck as I tumbled in. I caught my knee hard on the edge of the seat to the stern, cursing a good oath to control my tears. The sail had been rolled away but the oars were still inside, and I wasted no time in fitting them to the locks. The sooner I left the shore behind, the safer I'd feel. There would be time, later, to rest and to think. For now, I needed to send the boat through the water, taking myself away from Svolvaen, and danger. It was a struggle to breach the waves, tilting the blade to the right angle, but I was soon taking longer strokes, letting the boat glide onwards, with the great cliffs rising on either side.

I was shaken, weary and anxious but an old part of myself was awakening—the girl who'd climbed the tallest trees and swum in forest pools, who'd hunted rabbits and spun her own fate. If I were to survive, I'd need to be brave, and resourceful.

The moon appeared again, illuminating the sheer face of the crags. I was further along than I'd realized, moving parallel with the escarpment. Stilling the oars, I looked for an opening, wide and low and jagged either side—Helka's cave. I dipped the oars again, taking care not to drift close. Perhaps I'd gone too far. I might so easily have missed what I sought, in the faint, silvered light.

I saw the opening then, guarded by a jagged outcrop. Another moment and I'd be level. The swell rose as I approached—an upward surge, rushing into the inlet before the cave. It lifted the boat and tossed me towards unyielding stone.

I reached out my oar, endeavoring to push myself away, but the force of the waves was too violent. There was a judder as the bow connected, an alarming scrape and grind of buckling planks. I braced with a single oar, only to see it splinter and snap. Unthinkingly, I did the same with my hands, crying out as my palms scraped upon limpets.

The boat swayed, spinning to rasp upon the opposing rocks. I whimpered as the hull creaked, waiting for the rupture which would sink me. Water was about my ankles, the boat tilting. Grasping the remaining oar, I moved its blade desperately from one side of the boat to the other, propelling myself toward the cave's shelter.

26

Even as the sun rose high the next day, it remained cold within the cavern. I was drawn to the outer ledge in pursuit of warmth, of some touch of daylight. Watching the surf swell and surge, I sheltered unseen. Only one would guess I was here, and for her I waited. Helka would know what to say, what to do. She, I felt certain, would take my part.

What could I do but wait?

I found Helka's provisions—leather pouches of water, cheese and smoked ham. The cave's cool interior had preserved them well and how good they tasted, filling my mouth not just with flavor but with their solidity, with the pleasure of eating. I made myself chew slowly, passing each piece over my tongue. I didn't know how long I'd need them to last. Even eaten sparingly, they dwindled quickly.

Lying on my belly, I caught a sliver of shattered oar from the water. I thought to use it to prise limpets, as the birds did with their beaks, but the wood was already too soft to be of use. Eventually, I found a shell, the cast-off casing of a mollusc long-dead. It was a better tool, affording me several tiny mouthfuls, but those soft creatures clung tenacious to the rocks. In desperation, I smashed until my knuckles bled.

Scraping slimed algae and pliant seaweed from the rocks, my nails tore ragged. I pressed my mouth where my fingers were inept, tugging with my teeth, eager for any nourishment. Each swallow made me only thirstier. My brine-soaked mouth became parched dry amidst so much water. I was steeped in the sea, the stinging spray penetrating not just my clothes but my skin and my eyes. Its touch tormented my cracked lips.

I eyed the gulls soaring beyond the entrance of the cavern, wondering how they would taste, imagining the satisfaction of their flesh in my belly. None came near. It seemed more likely that they'd pick my bones than I theirs.

Long darkness and the muted day passed in the cavern's embrace. I curled upon the gnawing ache of hunger, shivering. Hiding my face in the crook of my elbow, I was wrapped in sweat despite the cold. The world had reduced to this damp place of stone and sea, to rock and water and the chill inside my bones.

Only in slumber was there relief. In my dreams, I joined the boys I'd played with in my childhood, swimming in the forest lake, gulping down great mouthfuls of sweet, fresh water. How we would run, and jump from the highest rocks, falling deep before kicking up to emerge, gasping and laughing.

I saw my grandmother, kissing me goodnight, my aunt, and the mother I'd barely known. Would I soon meet them all again? And Eirik. I dreamed of his soft kiss and of his arms, strong about me.

I dreamt, too, of entombment and engulfing dark, and woke to find it real. My chest, seizing tight, choked the air from my lungs— too thick to breathe.

One morning, I woke to an ominous gnawing within my left hand. There was infection, as I'd seen so many times: the affliction I'd avoided all these months. Across the width of my palm, the sore was livid, throbbing beneath the skin.

How much time had passed? Had Helka and Eirik been detained by Jarl Ósvífur? I clutched Eirik's amulet and invoked the gods. I did not wish to die, but to stay here would be my end.

I'd been a strong swimmer, once. Shouldn't I try? Swim for the shore; find some other place to hide. I sat upon the furthest point of the ledge, waited for a lull between the waves, and lowered myself into the sea.

27

Closing my eyes against the brightness all around, I kicked hard. I'd grown used to gloom and confinement. Now, the sky felt huge and the sun dazzling. I had to clear the perilous rocks; only then would I have a chance.

Almost immediately, the swell lifted me high then plunged low. Saltwater entered my nose and throat. I spluttered as the current swept me sideways. Scraping my elbow, I caught my breath in pain, but fought forward. I was almost dragged under before being hoisted upwards on a surging wave, which pushed me beyond the jagged outcrop.

I felt the difference at once and was filled with optimism. If I might now stay afloat, I could kick my way to shore. Yet, as I began to swim, I seemed to make no progress. The realization came to me in a flood of despair. How foolish I was! I'd never reach the shore, for the tide was on its way out, drawing me with it. I'd be swept out of the fjord, to the open sea.

In my panic, I kicked harder. I might, perhaps, make my way back to the rocks, drag myself hand over hand, returning to the cavern. That hope was in vain for the current was strong. Already,

I was drawing level with the next opening in the cliff—a smaller hollow, without visible ledge but also without rocks. I might take refuge there and wait for the turning tide. Summoning the last of my will, I thrashed through the water.

I entered green twilight, the water calm. This new cave stretched back further than I'd realized, ending in a shelf wide enough for me to sit upon, perhaps to lie. Algae grew thick upon the walls, fanning like hair where it touched the brine. I clutched a clump, pulling myself by its anchor, to heave myself from the sea.

Had I the strength, I might have cried but my quiet despair lodged in my throat. I fisted my left hand shut, not wishing to see what I knew grew there. My head throbbed and my limbs trembled. I could think no further than to rest, to sleep, curling upon myself as animals do, knowing themselves in the grip of sickness.

She came to me in my dreams. I lay in a lush meadow, the cornflowers tall around me and the sun warm. I closed my eyes to its glare. I heard her singing and then felt her gown brush my leg, from my ankle to my knee. There was nothing to fear for she was with me. I opened my eyes and saw her face, as lovely as it had ever been.

I woke to find my leg trailing in the water, long strands of green sweeping my skin. It had only been a fanciful reverie, yet I felt somehow comforted and renewed by Asta's appearance.

Something else had brought me from sleep. Not touch but sound, for there was a rushing noise, the low rumble of a storm and, closer, the sound of trickling water. The light was dim, for it was the first of the day, but enough to show me rain upon the sea and a low mist.

My body had no wish to move. Scraped, aching and fevered, my inclination was to close my eyes once more. Too long since I'd eaten, too long since I'd been warm or dry.

The tide would be turning but it would do me no good. My legs were leaden, and my body bruised; to swim seemed impossible. Straightening my arm brought a stab of pain. The abrasion on my elbow had crusted, then broken. The sore on my left palm itched. I opened it partially and winced. I clutched some algae, torn as I'd dragged myself from the water. Its slender strands were plastered to the lesion. I would examine it later, when I had the mind. There were nagging irritations elsewhere on my body that I refused to dwell upon. I'd no wish to look, for what good would it do?

I lay still, listening to a steady drip and splash. Helka had told me the cliffs were riddled with chasms and cracks, crevices through which water would travel. Perhaps if I could find the source, there would be fresh water to drink—enough to wet my mouth, at least. I was able to detect a fissure and a faint slant of light.

I groaned as I found my feet. My back and limbs protested but it was good to stand. If I allowed myself too much sleep, the temptation would be to never wake again.

The first section of the opening was the hardest to breach. The bones of my hip chafed awkwardly. Had I tried even a week ago, my flesh would have been too ample. There was a curve, obliging me to bend then crawl. I shuffled on my knees and knuckles. Hearing the trickle of water, I told myself it would be only a little further. If the tunnel forbade me final passage, it would be more than I could bear.

To my relief, the rock widened, and I emerged into a narrow column of space. I felt a change in the air—only a fraction warmer but certainly brighter. What I sought was flowing down the wall, forming a clear pool beneath. I plunged my lips, drinking greedily.

When I craned to look upwards, I almost laughed, for there was a distant chink of sky and a fresher smell. I'd found a hole through the rock, to the cliffs above. The gods had answered my prayers, showing me the way.

The rising granite had footholds and places my hands could grasp, but I feared for my strength. If I fell, my bones would surely find their rest here, hidden in the heart of the rock.

My left arm was in pain and my right gashed. Could I take the rough treatment of climbing? I felt less feverish, at least. I steeled myself to unfurl my fingers, knowing that I must inspect my palm. Algae had pressed into the tender flesh, preventing me from seeing the progress of the lesion. I lifted the strands, easing them from the sore. It was tender, but there was no ooze of pus, nor appearance of aggressive infection. I flexed my hand and blanched a little. However, the discomfort was bearable.

Not only had divine forces watched over me but nature, too, offering her bounty. I rested my head against the rock, giving silent thanks. Could this be what I'd been searching for, all these long months? I'd investigated many of the seaweeds along Svolvaen's shore but had never found this fine-threaded variety.

Perhaps it was true that even the worst misery served a purpose. The gods had led me here, surely, to find this remedy. It would be easy to return later, to bring a boat and fill it with enough to treat every person in Svolvaen many times over.

Nevertheless, it occurred to me that it would be unwise to reappear empty-handed. The charge of being a witch would mar the miracle of my survival in their eyes. If I brought the cure which they needed, perhaps it would convince them of my true intentions.

No algae grew in this small space where the spray did not reach. I grunted my discomfort as I crawled back through the fissure but was driven by the thought of Astrid, Ylva, Torhilda and her children. I'd collect what I needed and climb from this place. I'd cure the affliction for which others had blamed me and, in the process, save myself.

I tucked my apron upon itself, creating a pouch in front and behind, to stuff with the fine-threaded plant. With the torment of hunger nagging me, I pushed some into my mouth, making myself chew the thin strands. It would lend strength, I hoped.

A further length I twisted secure around my hand. My mind and heart were set.

28

The upward chasm provided ledges upon which I took respite, while bracing my feet on the opposing side. Several times, I hit my skull and lashed the air with curses, but an inner determination pushed me on. I set my jaw and inhaled deeply.

I'd come so far and would not fail.

No matter what lay in store, I'd perform this last act. Ylva would be released from the sores that blighted her young beauty, and Torhilde, too.

The sun was well past its zenith when my face met its warmth. I pressed my cheek to the moist grass, and my tears welled. I'd been lost to love, had been entombed, but I'd emerged into the light again.

After the quiet of the subterranean passage, I marveled at how the world hummed: bees hovering and dipping, crickets in the clover, and the chirrup of birds. The breeze carried the sound of every rustling leaf. A buzzard circled, sailing wild above the cliffs, observing everything in sharp detail—as I now did.

For some time, I basked in the late afternoon sunshine, letting it dry my clothes and revive my aching body. After dusk, I would creep down the hill, skirting behind the huts, to seek refuge in Astrid's home. Until then, I needed to conceal myself.

It was tempting to remain where I lay, but the desire to fill my belly won out. I crawled through the tufted clifftop grass to where the trees began. Wild strawberries grew there, and darker berries, which stained my trembling fingers as I crammed their sweetness to my mouth. Here, the moss was soft—a bed waiting for my head —and I found the oblivion of sleep.

It was night when my eyes opened again. My body was stiff, but my palm no longer felt tight and tender. My mind felt clearer than it had in days, and my forehead cooler. Had eating the algae released the fever from my blood? I marveled at its properties.

A bird shifted in the bushes, disturbing a fluttering of moths. I thought I heard a sigh. Was someone here? My neck prickled at the thought. There was no footstep through the undergrowth, no snapping of twigs. Peering deeper through the velvet dark, I saw nothing, but the conviction remained that someone breathed at my shoulder.

"Asta?" My voice was a quivering reed in this great forest. Huddling my arms close, I felt for the amulet at my neck, and my hand brushed the brooch Asta had given me.

I'd dreamt of her, in the cave; had felt her touch.

"Forgive me." My voice still quaked.

In the distance, an owl hooted and took flight.

29

I kept to the woods then crept through the long grass of the meadow, before approaching Astrid's house from behind. Though dusk had fallen, there seemed to be a gathering near the longhouse and I'd no wish to be seen.

On my second knock, Ylva opened the door.

"Who is it?" Astrid's voice carried from within.

Ylva gaped—at my wild appearance, I supposed, and at finding me still alive. I slipped inside, for it wouldn't do to stand too long.

"In the name of Freya!" Astrid leapt from her stool. In two bounds, she'd pulled me tight.

My tears sprung, for I'd been too much alone in the cold and dark. I'd near forgotten how it felt to be welcomed into a friend's arms.

"Don't speak." She looked me up and down. "Ylva, bring hot water and my green tunic… and some broth and bread."

I let her nimble fingers unfasten the straps of my apron, then stayed her hand.

"You've been collecting again—from the shore by the smell of it." She poked at the long strands of seaweed wrapped in the tuck of the apron's skirt.

I had to show her before she went any further, though I was loath to admit that I'd been unable to avoid the affliction. In that moment, I understood some fraction of the shame that Ylva had endured, and all the others who'd suffered with the blight.

Unfurling my palm, I picked off the strands of algae that clung, holding out my hand for Astrid to see. Even since that morning, it had improved, returning almost to its natural color.

She nodded quietly. "It was a wonder that you went so long without succumbing to the illness. It's just begun, has it?"

I choked back tears that threatened to bubble over. "It was much worse, and I had the fever, too."

"When you've some food inside you, it won't seem so bad. You can tell me everything when you're ready."

I did my best not to wince as she eased the damp tunic over my head. My shoulders were wrenched from the arduous climb, my arms still sore. Astrid tutted as she passed a warm flannel over my skin. There were other patches of skin, upon my back, which looked a little red, she told me, but none had blistered.

Astrid soothed me as she worked, bathing gently where I was most bruised. She wished even to spoon the broth to my lips, but I insisted on doing that for myself. It was thick with vegetables and meat; with each mouthful, I felt my strength returning.

"I knew you couldn't be dead." Astrid stood behind to comb my hair. "Though you don't look far off it, I have to say!" She wetted the slatted wood, doing her best not to pull.

"I rowed—" I began.

"I know about that." Astrid dropped her hand to my shoulder. "I went down to the harbor before dawn—before the fishermen, even. I couldn't see you by the pier. Then, I realized it was gone— the boat. You told me that Helka had sailed out with you, and I remembered. No one else would have dared to take it."

A clutch of fear seized me, for if Astrid knew then everyone did, surely. Why hadn't they gone searching? Wouldn't Gunnolf have commanded it?

She must have felt me stiffen. "There's no need to worry. Some would see no harm come to you." Taking up the comb again, she continued freeing the tangles.

"Anders suggested that we say his son found you disappeared and took Helka's boat, to see if your body were drifting. Everyone knows Halbert's headstrong. He's always been one for mischief. Halbert agreed immediately. He spun a tale about losing the boat on the rocks, sailing too close to the cliffs, then swimming back. Some have raised an eyebrow, but a piece of the hull washed ashore not long after."

My throat tightened again. Anders and Halbert were loyal to Eirik.

"What about the others? They still say I'm a witch?"

Astrid sighed. "Some do. Some don't. Some say the gods took you in punishment; others say they saved you. They spoke of little else, for a while..."

"And now?"

Pulling her fingers through my hair, she separated the lengths, making ready to plait them. "Other things seem more important. They're saying the jarl is out of favor with the gods; that he's not the man he was."

Astrid leaned closer to my ear. "He's forbidden anyone to speak of"—she hesitated, dropping her voice lower—"the *draug*."

It wasn't a word I'd heard before, but a chill passed over me. I searched Astrid's face.

"The restless spirit in human form. I told you of it, Elswyth."

She had, and the story had haunted me. After all that had happened, I had my own tales to tell, but those would wait.

Astrid began passing strands of my hair over and under, her fingers working methodically as she spoke, following the rhythm of braiding that required little thought. "Others have seen her, at the top of the hill. No one wishes to venture out after dark."

"No one?" I frowned. "I thought I saw people around the longhouse."

"Why, yes; today's different!" Astrid exclaimed, then her hands froze. "Forgive me, Elswyth. I thought this was why you'd come out of hiding. Because you'd seen; because you knew."

My heart jolted in that moment. I was aware of her fingers resuming their tidying of my hair, briskly forming a central plait and smaller ones either side.

Only when she'd finished, securing all with a strip of linen, did she again look into my eyes. "Eirik and Helka have returned to Svolvaen, with fine visitors. There's talk of marriage."

I'd prayed that Eirik would return. He had, but not for me.

The old grief stabbed, but I pushed it down.

Whatever secret wish I'd harbored, it was my discovery that had driven me back to Svolvaen. Despair would only hinder me.

I pointed at my bundled apron, discarded on the floor, long strands of green spilling out. "I had to come back, to show you. It's the remedy we've needed all along. "It's from the cave I sheltered in. The algae will help. I know it will."

Astrid's hands flew to her mouth. With a sob, she threw her arms about me.

Over Astrid's shoulder, I saw Ylva looking at us. As usual, she sat some distance away, but she'd heard everything. I'd never known her without her affliction. Perhaps, once, she'd been talkative and carefree. If so, she'd soon be again. My own hopes for happiness had been crushed but hers might yet be recovered.

I'd think of Eirik later. For now, I had a debt of friendship to repay.

I eased Astrid away from me, knowing it was time we got to work. I'd endured much but it hadn't been in vain. The gods had kept me alive, had given me time to reflect and the will to recover my courage. Just as Eirik was performing his duty, I'd do mine.

"We'll make the treatment together. I'll show you."

Ylva gave her assistance, grinding the pestle in the mortar, releasing the seaweed's healing juices. The plant had worked well as it was but how much more effective it would be once we'd prepared it.

"Soak your linen strips in the liquid and place them on each sore," I directed. "Steep the rest of the algae in heated water. Make a tisane and drink it down. Go afterwards to Torhilde and to the others. Act where I cannot."

Astrid's eyes shone wet as I borrowed her hooded cloak, drawing it close to my face to creep away.

I heard her as I closed the door behind me. "I knew you'd come back."

30

N ear the hill's summit, the mist was creeping between the dark trees, shifting and rolling, like a ghostly sea from which the ancient trunks rose. One might believe anything, see anything, on such a night.

I, too, was afraid, yet I continued. With my own eyes, I was determined to inspect Eirik's bride—the woman he'd chosen over me.

Light glimmered from two low windows, where the longhouse roof met its walls. The skins had been partially hooked aside to let the breeze enter. At the main entrance, two men stood sentry, their voices carrying low. They'd rather have been inside, no doubt, imbibing ale.

There was one other opening to the rear, and it was to this that I crept. Pressing close, I peered within. The hall was full, with Gunnolf's men and those who'd ridden out with Eirik. There were strangers, too; from Bjorgyn, I guessed.

Faline was wearing one of Asta's robes—yellow, embroidered with golden thread. It had suited my lady well. Faline's skin appeared sallow against its tone. For all the finery of the gown, she had no place at the table. Instead, she carried a jug, passing between the men to fill each cup.

Gunnolf barely looked at her, nor conversed with those on either side. Instead, his eyes, hollowed-dark, darted to the corners of the room. It gave me no pleasure to look at him. I'd been another woman in those days as his lover.

Helka was seated nearby but her attention was all upon the man to her left. He wasn't of the common build, being tall and slender, with fine features. His ear was keen to the words she shared with him and, when he leaned close, she closed her hand around his. She'd always kept men at a distance; this one, she did not.

I searched for Eirik. Would he appear different now he'd chosen a bride? There were many men worthy of a woman's attention, wearing the same sort of leather jerkin Eirik favored; men with blonde hair loose about their shoulders, and eyes sparkling in good humor.

And then my chest constricted. The girl sitting beside Gunnolf had the same, slight appearance as the man on Helka's left. Not yet ripe, as a woman should be on coming to her marriage bed, but with the promise of loveliness. This, surely, was Freydís, the daughter of Jarl Ósvífur—the alliance conceived by our jarl. The seat next to her was empty, though the place was set.

Helka rose. Moving behind her brother, she bent to his ear. Whatever she said, Gunnolf's expression remained distracted. He shook his head and waved her away, to which she frowned. Resuming her place, she remained standing, and took up her ale.

"Welcome, one and all, to the house of my brother, Jarl Gunnolf, and to Svolvaen: the home of courageous men and comely women."

I shifted a little, not wanting to miss anything, yet wishing also to keep myself hidden.

Helka's merry aspect faded for a moment. "It seems Eirik has some urgent business to attend to, but I speak for him when I say our long absence from Svolvaen was not without good reason." Here, she looked warmly at the man beside her.

"I half wonder if it were not Eirik's plan to be thrown from his horse, for our prolonged stay in Bjorgyn brought friendships which shall endure." Helka tipped her head towards the young girl beside Gunnolf. "Now, we look forward to the greatest of celebrations—the joining of our two clans through marriage."

At that, there was a stamping of feet.

I sunk to the grass beneath the window. There was no need to see more. I'd heard enough to pierce my heart.

What place was there for me now? Svolvaen's people did not want me; Eirik did not need me. Even were I to clear my name of the charges of witchcraft and poisoning, I could never bring myself to serve Eirik's new bride as I had Asta. If Eirik believed my innocence, he might find some man willing to make me his wife, but how could I live under that yoke? I'd never love another; would never be content unless the arms that held me were Eirik's.

I'd fought long to prove myself worthy of others' regard; fought to survive when all hope seemed lost. What had all my struggle been for? I'd helped others with my skills, but I couldn't heal my heart.

Perhaps contentment awaited me only in the next world. I thought of taking myself deep into the forest. I might simply lay down and close my eyes, and rest there forever more; or I could seek the cliff edge.

But how could I do such a thing? I'd come too far to give up.

I wouldn't succumb to the easy path. My story would not end here, but I needed to leave Svolvaen. I pictured myself wandering from place to place, offering my healing arts to the sick. Perhaps, one day, I would find those who'd truly welcome me. There might be a hearth, a home, and eventually, a husband. I was still young.

I felt a pang, knowing that I'd taken no farewell of Astrid. For that, I hoped she'd forgive me. There was only so much torment I could bear, and to remain here would be my undoing.

The night fog met me as I rose to higher ground. Laughter drifted up from the longhouse, sounds of shouts and clapping, dulled by the drifting mist.

I headed to my left, away from the sheer drop to the sea, but tumbling curls of white fast obscured the way. I was afraid to step blindly, having no wish to slip into some narrow crevice. A poor joke it would be, were I to find the crevasse through which I'd so recently climbed.

Better to crawl, so that my fingers would find any dangerous lip.

How cold it had become. Chill tendrils passed over my skin. I carried on, hearing the distant rumble of waves. The heels of my hands brushed bracken and the discarded nest of some hilltop bird. I winced as my knee found a stone's sharp edge.

And then all receded, and I was wrapped in silence.

My fingers touched something icy cold.

I wasn't alone.

Before me were slender feet, beneath the hem of a white robe, stained with soil.

I had no power to lift my head, to look upon the creature who stood before me. A cry rose in my throat but froze as surely as the breath and blood within my body. I attempted to speak her name, knowing it was she, but my voice abandoned me.

Choking back my tears, I recoiled, retreating from the one who had always been true to me and whom I had repaid so poorly.

It was another who broke the blanketing of the enfolding mist, another who ran, heedless, his voice strangled.

"My love. My love. Forgive me." Gunnolf's dark head bowed to kiss those feet.

In death, as in life, she was beautiful, but so pale, and her eyes no longer blue but black as the pit revealed beside her. As if risen from the grave, her hair was garlanded with leaves. Her cheek and hands were earth-smeared. She was a thing without the radiance of life yet moving and seeing.

He stepped to embrace her then gave a single cry. Consumed by the mist, he fell, to whatever emptiness lay below.

At once, another passed swiftly by me. Her scream was filled with both fear and rage. I shouted in warning, but it was too late. Perhaps Faline flung herself upon the ghostly form, or Asta reached to claim her.

They toppled as one into the gaping chasm.

31

The flame flickered in the lamp, showing me Helka's face.

"You're awake, thank the gods!" She lifted a cup to my lips. "Eirik found you, but no sign of our brother nor of Faline." She pushed hair from my eyes. "What happened, Elswyth?"

Where could I begin? Would it even make sense?

"I heard about Asta's death and their terrible accusation of you; of what my brother did." She squeezed my hand, resting above the furs on the bed. "How did you escape?"

I had no answer for that. The gods had saved me, I'd thought, or perhaps a hand had reached from beyond the grave.

"I knew it couldn't have been Halbert who took the boat. I guessed you must have gone to my cave."

I nodded but couldn't bring myself to recount what had occurred. I was so weary. What was to be gained from reliving those days? Couldn't I be left in peace?

"You're exhausted." Helka looked at me with anguish. "Forgive me, Elswyth. I wanted to sail out to find you with all haste —but I couldn't ignore the hospitality due to our guests. I had to wait. I would have sent Eirik alone, but I doubted he'd find the cave without my instruction. I planned to tell him of our secret as soon as the feasting was done. It meant a delay of only a few hours, but I was anxious nonetheless."

"It's of no matter." I sighed and returned the pressure of her fingers.

"Eirik wants to see you."

The mention of his name made the breath halt within my chest. How could I face him? My dignity remained, if little else.

"He refused to believe you were anything but innocent, Elswyth. Sylvi came forward today; she'd been afraid to speak, but she said she saw Faline putting something from an old pouch into Asta's *nattmal*."

It was some consolation, but I couldn't summon a joyful response.

"You were gone so long," I said, at last.

"Eirik's horse threw him as we were entering Bjorgyn. The injury wasn't severe, but I insisted travel was impossible. I kept him there far longer than was necessary."

"But, why?" This I couldn't understand.

"Selfish reasons." Helka's cheek reddened. "Leif... I needed to discover if there could be more between us... more than desire. I needed time, Elswyth, to know him, and for him to know me. Love comes by strange paths. I feel that he's been waiting for me, all this time. I still grieve for Vigrid but my heart has opened again."

"The man who sat beside you?"

This was something, at least. For Helka, I could be glad.

"You saw?" Helka shook away her confusion. "So, it was you he ran after? Gunnolf leapt from the table, shouted that he saw a face outside."

Perhaps it had been me; perhaps another.

Helka's voice was firm. "You must know, Elswyth, that Eirik was eager to return. The men of Bjorgyn lack his prowess; he might have bedded a dozen women, but none interested him." She leaned closer. "I made him stay, and he could hardly refuse since my choice would give him freedom."

Nothing made sense to me. "But, Freydís?"

"Ha! What of her?" Helka stifled her laughter. "She's pretty enough but hardly a match for Eirik. Even had he wanted her, her father would never have permitted it. He believes a man must demonstrate horsemanship above all; to fall from his mount before we'd even been presented to Jarl Ósvífur hardly boded well, and I made such a fuss of the injury! The jarl declared that no groom with the prospect of a limp would be worthy of his daughter, no matter the strength of his sword arm!"

"Then the marriage..."

"Is mine, of course!" Helka squeezed my hand again. "To Leif! Freydís is young but she has a stubborn streak. She begged to accompany us, to see the lands with which Bjorgyn was allying. Her father saw no reason to keep her from the adventure. The weather has been clement, and she carries herself well on horseback, as they all do."

"And Eirik?"

The curtain separating the box bed from the rest of the great hall pushed aside and he was suddenly standing over me, broad and strong, filling the space with his masculinity.

Helka retreated as Eirik wrapped me tightly in his embrace, holding me close. My cheek pressed to the warmth of his chest, while his own rested upon my head. My body remembered him, and my heart ached with the knowledge of my loss.

"My Elswyth," he murmured. When he released me, it was to draw my mouth upwards, in a kiss so deep that I forgot all but my love for him. "All those weeks I was away, my thoughts were with you; my heart was yours, always."

He pushed back the strands of my hair that had come loose. "What must you have endured! If I'd been here, I would never have allowed them to accuse you." His brows knitted in anger. "By the gods! How you are alive, I know not, but I thank Odin for it!"

He held my face between his hands, his voice fevered. "When they told me how they'd treated you, I wished to strike down Gunnolf where he stood! Only Helka's insistence stayed my sword."

I placed my hand over his, searching his gaze as he continued.

"I couldn't bring myself to sit at his table last night. I was in the stable while they ate. Helka told me she would come for me as soon as she was able—that she had something to tell me."

There was so much I wished to say. Above all, I needed to tell Eirik of my errors and ask his forgiveness. I was not blameless. He had wronged me while following his sense of duty while I had chosen my path wholly in anger. My resentment and wounded pride had led me only into further pain.

He tightened his hold, as if never to let me go. His voice broke with emotion, husky with longing and all that lay unspoken between us.

"Elswyth, I must have you—for my bed, for my pleasure and your own, to bear my children as my wife, for all the time given to us by the gods. Whatever is past, we must forget. From this day forward, we shall promise to love one another, and this will be all that matters."

In answer, I raised my face and took another kiss. For what the gods decreed would be, and I knew that I would always be safe in the arms of the man who loved me above all others.

EPILOGUE

It was to be a summer of marriages, not only mine to Eirik, and Helka's to Leif. Ylva was among them; she gave her hand not to the young man who'd spurned her but to Halbert, the blacksmith's son. I was glad of it, and for all the happiness that ripened, along with Svolvaen's crops. We were healing, in many ways.

I sometimes thought of Gunnolf, and Faline, free at last, of ambition, envy, and resentment. I hoped they were at peace, and Asta, too.

Svolvaen gained a new jarl, and Eirik's shoulders bore the honor well, though he mourned the loss of his brother. No matter the many grievances between them, they had been blood-bound.

It shamed me to admit my many follies to Eirik. I'd lost all sense of myself in trying to destroy the last ruins of my love. I'd been half mad with remorse over Asta's death. Gunnolf and I, both, had allowed the worst of ourselves to reign in those dreadful weeks.

Eirik sat in silence as I spoke. I feared he'd be unable to forgive but he blamed himself more than I.

The cause of the sores was never known, but we'd found our cure. It would take time, as I'd foreseen, for me to counter mistrust. None called me 'witch' or 'murderess'—or, at least, not to my face. I told my story, as best I could, but not all of what had occurred could be explained. The workings of the gods and those places beyond our earthly realm are not ours to fathom.

Each night, Eirik stroked my hair until I fell asleep. In his arms, I believed there would be no bad dreams for, whatever the future held, we would face it together.

Ready for the next installment of the 'Viking Warriors' series?

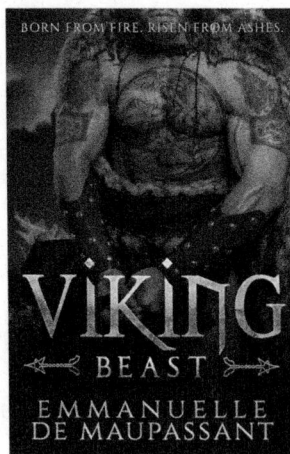

A reputation built upon ruthless savagery.
A leader reveling in bloodshed and conquest.
A man bent on revenge.

Newly wedded to Eirik, now jarl of all Svolvaen, I carry the baby we both long for.

But Svolvaen's fiercest enemy will not grant us peace.

Falling into the hands of the Beast, there is no escape.
I must summon all my strength.
Without it, I won't survive.

'Viking Beast' is a novel of love, betrayal, secrets and redemption.

GLOSSARY

to go 'a-viking' – to go raiding/marauding
blót – ritual sacrifice
dagmal – morning meal
draug – the returning dead, restless due to some injury suffered in life
draumskrok – a nonsensical dream
hörgr – altar stone
huldra – a seductive female forest spirit luring men to become her slave or lover, or to bring their death
jarl – the chieftain of the community
Jörmungandr – the serpent which encircles the Earth and, on releasing its tail, will begin the events of *Ragnarök*
Jul – the New Year festival
karl – a free man within the community, serving the jarl as his leader
nattmal – late afternoon/early evening meal
Ragnarök – the great battle between the gods and the final destruction of the world, leading to rebirth

Ostara – the spring festival
skald – a travelling storyteller/bard
thrall – a slave (often captured during raids)

ABOUT THE AUTHOR

Emmanuelle de Maupassant lives in the Highlands with her husband and her hairy pudding terrier, Archie, (connoisseur of squeaky toys and bacon treats).

For behind the scenes chat, you may like to join Emmanuelle's Boudoir, on Facebook.

FURTHER WORKS

BY EMMANUELLE DE MAUPASSANT

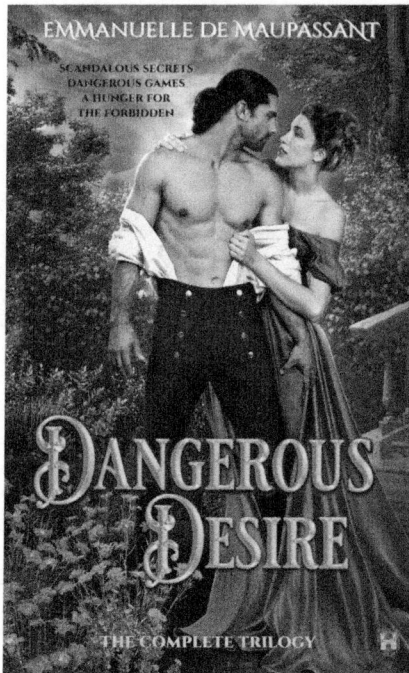

Dangerous Desire
One encounter changes everything.

When the Earl of Rancliffe suffers humiliation at the hands of the mysterious Mademoiselle Noire, he vows revenge. But his anger soon becomes obsession, as she leads him into ever more dangerous games.

As cruel as she is beautiful, Mademoiselle Noire has no intention of revealing her true identity, nor of entangling her heart.
But in a world of vice and dark desire, what does her heart secretly yearn for?

Devour this boxed set, which comprises all three darkly sensual romances from the 'Dangerous Desire' trilogy.

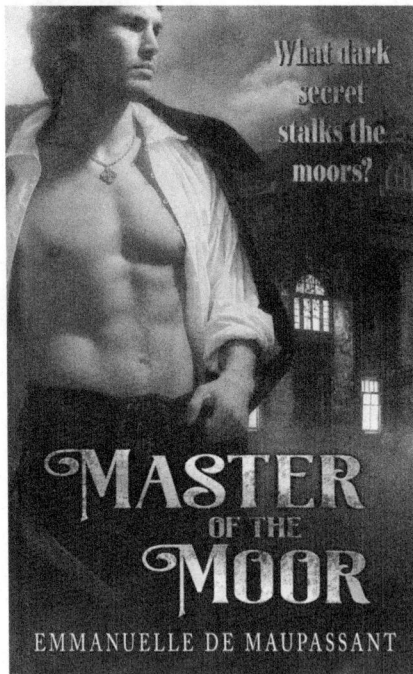

Master of the Moor

What happens when a brooding hero meets an unscrupulous heroine, who'll do anything to make a suitable match?

The winds howl and mist creeps over the dark cliffs of Dartmoor as the enigmatic Mallon and ravishing Geneviève meet at Wulverton Hall.

❧

Discover Emmanuelle's 'Lady's Guide' series: historical romance brimming with mystery, passion and intrigue.

The Lady's Guide to a Highlander's Heart

The Lady's Guide to Mistletoe and Mayhem

The Lady's Guide to Escaping Cannibals

The Lady's Guide to Scandal

The Lady's Guide to Deception and Desire

The Lady's Guide to Tempting a Transylvanian Count

NINE CONQUERING REASONS TO SURRENDER

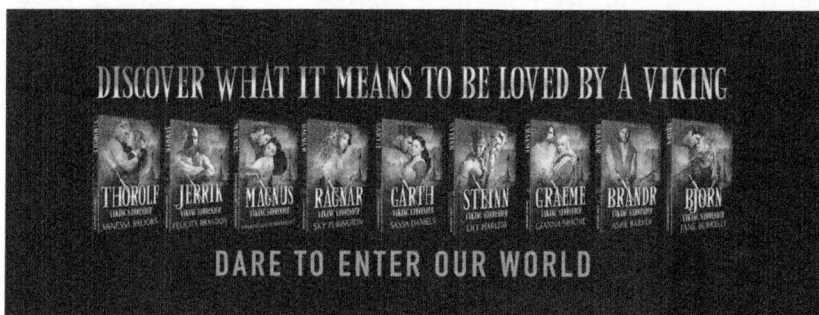

DISCOVER WHAT IT MEANS TO BE LOVED BY A VIKING

THOROLF · JERRIK · MAGNUS · RAGNAR · GARTH · STEINN · GRAEME · BRANDR · BJORN

DARE TO ENTER OUR WORLD

Dare to Enter our World

Battle-hardened and broad-chested, with shoulders built for carrying you to bed, these Vikings are pure muscle, and pure determination.

Delivered into Viking hands, the brides of Achnaryrie now belong to their conquering masters but, as wedding nights bring surrender to duty, will fierce lovers also surrender their hearts?

The Highland wilderness is savage, life is perilous, and the future uncertain, but each Viking has sworn protection, and there are no lengths to which a man will not go to safeguard the woman he loves.